Englehart Room
A107

Judith Bernie Strommen

# Champ Hobarth

*Henry Holt and Company / New York*

94-02

Henry Holt and Company, Inc.
*Publishers since 1866*
115 West 18th Street
New York, New York 10011

Henry Holt is a registered
trademark of Henry Holt and Company, Inc.

Library of Congress Cataloging-in-Publication Data
Strommen, Judith Bernie.
  Champ Hobarth / by Judith Strommen.
    p.   cm.
  Summary: Marty, a perennial failure in a family of high
achievers, finds something to fight for when his love of a stray
dog takes him to the local animal shelter and he discovers
the plight of the many homeless pets there.
  [1. Dogs—Fiction.   2. Animals—Treatment—Fiction.
  3. Self-perception—Fiction.]   I. Title.
  PZ7.S9218Ch   1993
  [Fic]—dc20      92-35317

ISBN 0-8050-2414-X

First Edition—1993

Printed in the United States of America on acid-free paper. ∞
10  9  8  7  6  5  4  3  2  1

*For my parents,*
*Jack and Arline Bernie,*
*who took in the basket.*

My thanks to the residents, the staff, and the volunteers of the Tri-County Humane Society in Saint Cloud, Minnesota, for their friendship to me at a time when I needed it most. They're heroes, every one.

My deepest admiration to Executive Director Vicki Lynn Davis and Shelter Manager Laurie Gerard for their tireless devotion to the mission of the society: to provide humane treatment for all living creatures. Their hearts, their voices, their lives speak eloquently for those who cannot.

My appreciation to Don Lemke, co-owner of Clearwater Interiors, who shared his knowledge, his experience, and his furniture store with me.

# Contents

1 / The Zilch   1

2 / The Incredible Shrinking Kid   8

3 / Champ Hobarth   17

4 / The Big Question   25

5 / Mr. Chu's Cookies   33

6 / Incognito   44

7 / Jail   50

8 / Super Double-Top Extra Cheese   60

9 / The Family   67

10 / Twenty-five Hours a Day   77

11 / The Rescuer   88

12 / The F & A   96

13 / Garbage   105

14 / Walking Billboards   117

15 / Operation Shutdown   128

16 / Back to Krypton   139

17 / Discoveries   146

18 / Home   162

Epilogue: The Johnson Falls *Gazette*   179

# Champ Hobarth

# 1

# The Zilch

Inch by inch Marty Hobarth eased himself out onto the high diving board at the Johnson Falls municipal swimming pool. His feet scraped its sandpapery surface. His heart pounded. His arms, raised like wings for balance, teetered in the breeze.

When he reached the end and there was nothing in front of him but air, he stared down at the ice-blue water below him. He tried to swallow, but the spit was gone from his mouth.

What was he doing trying out for the diving team? Who did everybody want him to be? Mr. Olympics?

"Hey, Hobarth! You about ready?" It was the coach.

Marty looked down and saw him write something on his clipboard. Probably something like "Forget Hobarth. The kid's a zilch."

Well, maybe he was a zilch. But then nobody had bothered to tell him he'd have to try out from the *high* dive.

He gave a small, testing pump to the end of the board, to show the coach he was almost—sort of—ready. Instantly the board dipped and then sprang up. He flung his arms out to steady himself.

*1*

Near the coach stood the other kids who were trying out. David Bock was in the middle of them, huddled in his orange towel. David, who'd been in Marty's class at school and thought everything was a piece of cake. David had already done his dive and, Marty knew, easily made the team. He was the one who should be a Hobarth. He'd fit right in.

David waved up at him.

Marty did not wave back. He didn't want to lose his balance.

Of course, he'd been on the high dive lots of times before . . . to do cannonballs. But it didn't seem so high up when you were just doing cannonballs. What if he belly flopped right there in front of everybody? What if he hit the water so hard, it slapped the skin right off his body and they had to call the ambulance and carry him out on a stretcher?

His picture would be on the front page of the *Gazette*. Underneath it would say:

> Lawrence Martin Hobarth, also known as "Marty the Zilch," performed an Olympic belly flop at the municipal pool today. Son of John and Liz Hobarth, brother of Francine the superbrain, Marty the Zilch was unable to speak to our reporter at the scene. His lips were stuck to his teeth. But schoolmate David Bock said no one was surprised by the accident. Lawrence Martin, he explained, was not good at anything.

Marty frowned as he curled his toes tighter around the edge of the board. He listened to the thumping that had started up in his ears and he looked away from David, out across the pool. He saw people splashing in the shallow end and people swimming laps. People lying in the sun and people playing cards. Everyone was having fun but him.

He gulped a fast breath and tried to wriggle the jitters out of his fingertips. In the park beyond the pool fence, things looked quieter. Just trees and grass and a big dog loping along the walking trail.

He wished he was out there, with the dog. Or he wished he was at home. Anywhere. Even the dentist's office would be better than this.

"Hobarth!" It was the coach again.

Marty nodded. If he didn't hurry up and do it, he was going to chicken out. Just like his sister said he would.

Except he wasn't even sure he could chicken out. He glanced quickly over his shoulder, trying to see the board behind him, but he couldn't quite. Which meant, if he decided to chicken out, he would have to back up without seeing, in a perfect straight line, or he would fall off and be a splat on the cement.

Which meant he had to dive.

He raised his arms over his head. He clasped his fingers together, pointing them toward the sky, and sucked in air until his lungs were filled to bursting. He took one last look at the park, then slammed his eyes shut. He pictured himself doing a splashless, smooth-as-a-knife dive. Then, with a lurch of his stomach, he let himself go.

But it was wrong!

Instantly, it was *wrong*!

His arms were still pointing to the sky! His feet were aiming down! He was not diving! He was going in feet first, arms up. Like the victim of a holdup.

Before he could open his eyes (as if seeing could fix things!) his pointing toes hit the icy water and he slipped in, smooth as a knife. The noise of the world vanished as a rush of bubbles closed over his head.

He shot down through the swirling water with the speed of a torpedo. Chlorine stung the inside of his nose. Muffled sounds of underwater filled his ears. He squeezed his hands into fists.

How could anybody be so dumb? In front of so many people?

When his feet scraped bottom, he did what he had to do. He gave a push up. Because if he hid down there, for even half a minute, they'd send a life-guard in after him. That would be even worse.

He let himself float to the surface. When his head broke through to the air, he gulped it, bobbing in the middle of the deep end, and opened his eyes.

There they were. David, the coach, all the other kids. Watching him.

Grimly, he turned toward the ladder and began a slow dog paddle to the side of the pool. When he grabbed the top rung of the ladder, David squatted down in front of him. His towel dipped into the water.

"Geez, Marty," he said. "What'd ya do that for?"

"I don't think he meant to," said Ann Louise Miller, in a loud whisper. "It's so embarrassing."

Behind Ann Louise somebody giggled.

And Marty felt his face heat. Without a word to David or Ann Louise or anybody, he hoisted himself out of the pool. What he needed to do was get out of there and never come back. Not ever.

But the coach waved him over.

"Would you like to try again, Hobarth?" he asked when Marty stood in front of him, dripping.

At just that moment the breeze touched Marty's wet skin (which was still there, he reminded himself) and sent tremors down both arms. Try again? Marty shook his head no.

"You sure?"

Dead sure, Marty wanted to say. He nodded instead.

Coach looked at him for a long moment and then went back to his clipboard. "All right then, Hobarth. Have a good summer. Sanders? You're next."

Marty snatched up his towel and his shoes and pressed through the group of kids without looking at any of them. Somebody called after him, but he kept on going. His eyes burned from the pool chlorine.

He hurried past some sunbathers, his left foot bumping their bottle of lotion. "Hey, watch it!" one of them yelled as he rushed by.

His face was steaming now, and he dried it with a swipe of his towel. He really was a Zilch. Zilch with a capital Z, which was Embarrassing with a capital E, and not only because of the people at the pool.

There was his dad to think about. But he didn't want to think about his dad. Not yet. And then there was his sister Francine. When she heard the news, she'd write a letter to Mom, who was in Mexico studying things. Then she'd get on the phone with her finky friends. Lawrence Martin bombed again, she'd tell everyone. How Embarrassing.

He reached the pool entrance and slid through the creaky turnstile. He followed the sidewalk until it ended, at the stairs that led to the parking lot. He looked behind him to see if anyone had followed.

No one had.

So he slumped down on the top step, dropped his shoes, and bent over to loosen the laces. As he shoved his left foot in, the dog he'd seen in the park came lumbering over the hill.

When the dog spotted him, he changed course and trotted over. His fur was speckled with every dog color Marty'd ever seen. On his side one large brown splotch looked like it belonged on a map.

But he, Marty, didn't have time to watch dogs. He needed to get out of there!

He was about to reach for his other shoe when the dog arrived. With a woosh of tail he plopped down on the step in front of Marty and the shoe disappeared under a tangle of fur. The dog looked at Marty. Then he lifted one paw.

It was huge.

In fact, the whole dog was huge. Plus his ears sagged. His eyes drooped. And he smelled like a swamp.

"Hey," said Marty. "You're on my shoe."

The dog pushed at Marty's arm with his paw.

"You wanna shake hands with a zilch?" asked Marty. "Is that it?"

The dog tipped his head, as if he understood, and it reminded Marty of a dog he'd seen in a movie once. A dog that could almost talk.

The paw pressed, insistent, against Marty's wrist.

"Okay. But then you gotta move." Marty took the giant, warm paw in his hand and shook it. He watched the dog's eyes twinkle.

"Guess you don't know about zilches, huh?" he asked, half expecting an answer.

But at that moment a horn honked.

Marty turned.

It was his dad. He'd pulled into the parking lot in his store van, and Marty hadn't even noticed. HOBARTH'S F & A it said in blue letters across the side. FURNITURE AND ACCESSORIES FOR EVERY HOME.

"Hey, champ!" his dad called up to him through the open driver's-side window. "How'd it go?"

# 2

# The Incredible
# Shrinking Kid

**M**arty walked down the pool steps to the parking lot, the dog close behind. When he reached his dad's van, he set one foot on the running board and forced a smile. "Dad. Hi. What are you doing here?"

"I wanted to watch you dive, but I see I've missed it. A customer came in just as I was leaving."

"Gee." Marty tried hard to sound sorry. "That's too bad."

"How was it? And where is everyone else? David Bock tried out too, didn't he?"

Marty's dad had met David and his parents the night of the school open house. He liked David.

"David?" Marty pushed the lock button on the van's door down and then pulled it up. Down and then up. Click, click. If his dad saw David, he'd want to say hello. He'd say, "How'd it go, Dave?" He'd want the details.

"He left already, Dad. They all did. I'm the last one."

Marty did not look at his dad when he spoke. He

focused instead on the small blue squares in his dad's shirt, because nobody, of course, had gone anywhere yet. But if his dad knew that, he'd want to stay. He'd want to go up and meet not just David but all the divers. He'd want to introduce himself to the coach. The thought of it made Marty's stomach churn.

He looked away, into the van's side mirror, and saw the bike rack, which was only a few feet away. It was full with the bikes of all the divers, including his own. He couldn't let his dad see that! Quickly he covered the mirror with one arm.

"Well then." Mr. Hobarth drummed his fingers against the steering wheel. "Hop in. I'll drive you home."

Marty beamed. So what if he had to come back for his own bike? He hurried around the front end of the van.

The dog followed.

Marty grabbed the door handle to climb into the van. "Stay, dog!" he said.

But the dog wouldn't. He pressed closer, his tail wagging, as if he expected to ride along. When Marty opened the door, the dog slipped past him and lunged into the front seat.

Marty watched the dog give his dad a slurpy chomp on the sunglasses. As if they were old friends.

"Marty!" his dad called from somewhere behind the mass of fur.

"I'll get him, Dad."

It took the two of them, Marty pulling and his dad pushing, to get the dog off the front seat, out of the van, and back onto the blacktop.

"He's big as a moose," said Mr. Hobarth. "And he needs a bath. He ought to have I.D. tags on too. It's a city ordinance."

Marty scanned the park for anyone who looked like he'd just misplaced his dog. He listened for a voice calling. But there was no one. (And thankfully, no divers!)

He opened the van door again, but this time just enough to slide himself in sideways. When he yanked the door shut, the dog stood on his hind legs, outside the van, and whined.

"Get him down, Mart," said Mr. Hobarth. "Before he scratches the paint."

Marty looked into the dog's begging eyes and wished he could stay and pet him awhile. But he had to hurry. "Sorry, fella," he said. Then he added fiercely, for his dad's benefit, "Get down!"

When the dog did, Mr. Hobarth stepped on the accelerator and the van pulled away from the curb. Marty buckled his safety belt and leaned back against the seat. He looked out the side mirror for the dog, but the only thing he could see was himself. Hair dripping, eyes red.

The front seat was hot. Marty's skin stuck to the vinyl upholstery. He should have laid his towel down first, before he got in, but in the big hurry he hadn't thought of it. He hadn't thought about how he was going to explain things to his dad, either. And now they were alone together. Where would he even start? He bunched the towel into a ball on his lap and tried to think.

His dad switched the turn signal, and the van rolled out onto the boulevard. Behind Marty's seat tools clanked. A box slid across the floor.

"Okay now, champ," said his dad. "Tell me."

Marty twisted a handful of the towel. Maybe he should start with how high up the diving board was. Or how he'd forgotten his nose plugs.

"I bet you were great," Mr. Hobarth said, not waiting for an answer. "I bet we've got an Olympic diver in the family."

Marty squinted against the glare off the dashboard. This was not going to be easy. "I don't think so, Dad."

"Come on now, Mart. Remember what we talked about?"

Of course he remembered. He'd heard it a million times.

His dad said it anyway. "If you don't expect to succeed, you never will."

"I know, Dad. But—"

"But what?"

Marty swallowed. "But I didn't exactly do real good."

Mr. Hobarth dismissed Marty's words with a wave of his hand. "So what if you weren't perfect? You'll work at it. You'll get better. Do you think I won the first marathon I ran?"

"No, Dad. It was your fifth."

His dad smiled over at him. "The key here is attitude. You've got to start thinking like a winner, Marty. Like your sister does when she competes in the spelling contests."

Marty thought about how Francine's picture had been on the front page of the *Gazette* the day she won the regionals, and he felt himself begin to shrink.

He wiggled his toes against the wet insides of his tennis shoes. Pretty soon, he imagined, his feet wouldn't reach the floor mat. Pretty soon he wouldn't be able to see over the dashboard. Pretty soon he'd get strangled by the seat belt. He was turning into the incredible shrinking kid.

He looked out the window and saw boulevard trees and kids on bikes and a lady pushing a baby stroller. Everything seemed normal sized outside, which meant it was happening just in the van.

"Marty? Are you listening to me?"

Marty shook his head and drips of pool water showered down from his hair.

"I said, your mother will be so pleased you're on the team. She worried you wouldn't keep busy this summer."

Marty tried to move in the seat, but his back was stuck to the vinyl. If only his mom was home. Then he could tell *her* about messing up the dive (She wouldn't get so upset!) and *she* could tell his dad for him. But no. She was out digging up dirt at some place in Mexico that he couldn't even spell. Hunting for old bones and pottery with some people from the college.

He was going to have to handle things himself.

His dad patted his arm. "Don't look so unhappy, Mart. You've got an opportunity here, not a problem. If you don't get discouraged and give up."

"But, Dad—"

"No buts, Marty. Not this time."

Marty squeezed the towel in his lap. His dad was remembering other times. Like the hockey tryouts, when he'd cut his chin on the ice and gotten stitches instead of a place on the team. Or the one week he played basketball. Or his math quizzes at school. There were a lot of possibilities.

He peered at his reflection in his dad's sunglasses. He was shrinking, all right.

They turned onto their own street, Fox Lane, and the tools behind Marty jangled. The box slid back across the floor. When Mr. Hobarth pulled up next to the curb in front of their house, he patted Marty on the shoulder. "Put a smile on, champ," he said. "It's going to be a great summer."

Marty opened his mouth to say something, but his dad waved him out. "Gotta run."

Marty pushed on the door handle. Then, letting the skin on his back pull away from the vinyl seat, he climbed out of the van.

His father gave the horn a see-you-later toot and drove off down the street. Marty stood on the curb and watched him go. Hugging the towel to his stomach, he shuffled across the front lawn. The foam inserts in his shoes squished like sponges. On a tree limb above him a jay scolded.

"Thanks a lot, bird," he said.

He walked past his mother's geranium pots to the back steps and climbed them. Each foot weighed a ton. He pulled open the screen door and stepped into the kitchen.

Oh goody. Francine was home.

She was on the phone, twisting strands of hair around one finger. "Just a sec, Allison," she said, frowning. "The p-a-i-n is home."

As if he couldn't spell.

She pointed the telephone at him like a weapon and said, "Don't listen."

"Don't worry." He walked past her, scuffing his shoes against the wood floor, and went up the stairs to his room.

The mattress coils creaked as he flopped across the bed. He closed his eyes and saw himself back at the pool, as if a video tape were running inside his head. He watched himself jump off the diving board. He listened to everybody laugh. They all thought he should have a clown suit on he was so funny.

He propped himself up on one elbow. Usually, no matter what else was happening, he felt better once he got to his room. Only it wasn't working this time. In fact, he was now feeling worse. And his pillow smelled like chlorine.

He got up and shuffled over to the terrarium that sat on his bookcase shelf. He knelt in front of it. The tree frogs were suctioned to the side wall, baking in the warmth of the incandescent bulb. Godzilla was on the electric rock.

"Hey, Zill."

The chameleon turned his head lazily to the side and focused one eye on Marty.

Marty watched Godzilla's undisturbed, even breathing.

Lizards were lucky. They didn't have to think like winners. Or try out for teams.

Marty lifted the terrarium lid. Gently he scooped Godzilla out and set him on the back of his hand. The underside of the chameleon's belly and the tips of his feet were dry and cool.

Marty wished he could stay there, with Godzilla, the rest of the day.

But his bike was at the pool. And his dad was at the store, probably telling all his customers that his son was an Olympic diver.

He sat down on the floor and let Godzilla pad lightly up his arm. He should have told his dad the truth right away. Before he'd even gotten into the van. Before his dad had started talking.

But he hadn't. He'd chickened out.

Which meant he'd better bike downtown to the

store and get it over with. Because the longer it went, he knew from experience, the worse it would get. The not telling. And he certainly couldn't do it at home, over the phone, in front of Francine.

He leaned against the bookcase. He'd have to go back to the pool to get his bike first. David and all the other kids would probably still be there. He'd see them. They'd laugh.

It was going to be horrible.

Plus what if his dad made him go back and try it again?

He eased Godzilla back into the terrarium and closed the lid. Maybe shrinking wasn't such a bad thing, really. Maybe, if you did it enough, you could disappear altogether.

# 3

# Champ Hobarth

It took a while for Marty to walk himself
back to the pool. He went the long way, past the
Heights apartment complex and a laundromat, past
Li'l Putt Golf and the Jiffy Mart, instead of cutting
through the middle of his own neighborhood. Because a guy didn't always feel like seeing a lot of
people he knew. Plus it took time to get yourself
ready to tell your dad you bombed again.

When he reached the dirt service road that ran
along the back of the pool park, the sun was directly overhead. His hair had dried and his shoes
had stopped squishing and he wished he'd carried
his canteen or a bottle of pop.

He dug through his pockets, hoping maybe he'd
left a piece of gum in them, but he hadn't. So he
pulled his hands out and hooked his thumbs
through the front belt loops of his jeans as he
walked the tire grooves in the road.

Even from back there the racket from the pool
was loud: the hollering and the splashing, the bleat
of lifeguards' whistles. Everybody was still having
fun. He kicked at a clod of dirt.

Across the road from him were bushes that grew like a wall along the side of the parking lot. If he'd figured right, the bike rack ought to be just on the other side of it at about this spot. Which meant he could slip through it, grab his bike, and be gone without having to walk past all the kids at the pool who'd watched him jump.

He wiped away a line of perspiration from his upper lip. Of course, he'd have to see everybody sooner or later. Some of them were friends. But later was always better in situations like this.

With a quick glance in each direction, he crossed the road and stepped into the row of bushes.

It was a jungle. Thick and prickly and loaded with perfumy purple flowers that made him want to sneeze. Bugs hummed like a chorus of tiny kazoos.

He pushed branches away from his face, but they snapped back after he passed them and scraped at his ears. He tripped on roots.

After he'd picked his way through, he pulled back a cluster of the flowers and peeked out.

The bike rack was only a few feet in front of him. He saw his own bike at the other end.

He started to step out when he heard voices. Instantly he pulled his foot in and watched from behind a clump of leaves.

Girls.

They'd come from the pool. They'd probably seen his performance on the diving board. They'd probably laughed, too. If he stepped out, they'd remember him. Then they'd want to know, what was he doing in the bushes? Spying?

He swatted at something on his ankle and wished they'd hurry up.

They didn't. They had hair to comb and back-packs to put on and plans to make. Somebody named Leanne was telling about how she was visiting Johnson Falls for the summer. About how much hotter it was in Kansas. It was a long story.

Marty rubbed his back against a branch and won-dered what his dad was doing right then. Selling a dining room set, maybe. And boasting to the cus-tomer about his Olympic son.

The thought made him feel jumpy. Some kind of beetle zinged past his face, and his neck was begin-ning to itch. (The bushes weren't poison ivy, were they?) He ought to forget about the girls and just go get his bike.

He lifted one foot, to step out, when the girl named Leanne said, "Look!"

Marty looked.

The police department's Animal Control truck had pulled into the lot. Marty watched it wind slowly through the lines of parked cars until it moved out of his view. A fat branch was in the way. He stepped up on a root and looked out over it.

The truck came to a stop in front of the steps that led up to the pool. A woman in a dark uniform climbed out from behind the wheel.

What was Animal Control doing at the pool? Releasing squirrels? Rescuing ducks?

Marty watched her open the back of the truck. She didn't lift out a cage. She wasn't carrying a net. She had a leash.

"Animal jail," said the Leanne girl.

"Oh no," said another.

"Oh yes," said the third. "I bet she's after the big spotted dog."

Big spotted dog?

Marty gripped the branch. Did she mean the giant dog he'd met earlier? The one who could almost talk?

He leaned farther out and watched the woman walk past the bike rack and up the steps toward the pool. Then, suddenly, the branch snapped. He tumbled out of the hedge and landed sitting up on the blacktop.

The Leanne girl stared down at him. "Where'd you come from?" she asked. "You got flowers on your head."

Marty stood up. He brushed his hands through his hair and purple petals fell shimmering to the ground. "What big spotted dog?"

She pointed in the direction of the pool. "That one."

It was the giant dog, all right. He was trotting down the steps next to the woman in the uniform, his tail waving like a parade flag. And he was on the leash.

The girl jabbed Marty with her elbow. "It isn't fair!" she cried. "Somebody should *do* something!"

She was right.

Marty bolted for the truck. "Wait!" he yelled as he ran. "Wait!"

The woman in the uniform turned. The dog, who now had his front paws on the tailgate of the truck, turned too. When he saw Marty, his tail began to wag the whole rest of his body.

Marty banged his shin on the bumper of the truck as he skidded to a stop. "Wait," he said again, over the noise of the idling engine. "Please."

He bent to catch his breath. He could feel the dog—and the woman—looking at him. They were waiting for what he was going to say next. Only he didn't know what he was going to say next. He'd never done this before.

He rubbed the lump starting on his leg. From inside the back compartment of the truck, he could hear whining and a yip and the fussing wail of a cat. Nobody was having any fun at all.

He limped around the tailgate and then stood, eye to eye with the dog. "Hold it a minute," he whispered. "I gotta think."

The dog breathed in his face.

"City hall had a complaint about him," said the woman. "Is he yours?" She had a handkerchief and was wiping her forehead. "If he is, just take him home and keep him there. I've got two more calls to make and I'm already almost full."

She nodded her head toward the back of the truck.

Marty did not want to look in the back of the truck. But he couldn't help it. A red dog stared back at him through the metal squares of a cage.

Marty swallowed hard. What was going to happen to that dog? And what about the cat? He'd heard a cat, too, hadn't he?

"Is he yours?" The woman was waiting.

Marty placed his hand on the dog's large speckled head. "Yes," he heard himself say. "He's mine."

The words caught in his throat, and he had to cough to clear them out. What in the world did he think he was doing? His family didn't have dogs. Not even little clean ones. Forget a monster like this!

"Where's his collar?"

"His collar?"

"Yes. He has to wear a collar. He has to have tags."

Of course he had to wear a collar. Any dunce knew that. He was a dog, for heaven's sake.

The line of perspiration was back along Marty's upper lip, and he wiped at it with his arm. A picture of his dad floated up in his mind but he shoved it away. "His collar's at home," he said. "It broke."

The woman tucked the handkerchief in her pocket. "He's had his shots, hasn't he?"

"Shots." Marty ran his foot along a crack in the blacktop. "Oh yes. He gets lots of shots. All the time."

"I can see he's still a puppy. But how old is he?"

A *puppy*? Marty felt his jaw drop.

The lady shaded her eyes from the sun. "I suppose he's a little over a year?"

"Um, that's it. A little over a year." Just how big was this puppy going to get?

The woman hesitated. "What's your name?"

Marty told her.

"I really should give you a ticket, Marty. You've got to take responsibility if you're going to have a pet. And puppies need extra care."

Marty winced. If he did have a dog (or a puppy) it would never *want* to run away. He'd feed it and play with it and never let it out of his sight. It wouldn't smell like a swamp, either. But he couldn't say any of that. He had to let the woman think he was a dunce.

"Can you promise me this won't happen again?"

"No. I mean yes. I mean no, it won't happen again." How many lies had he told in the last two hours?

The woman knelt in front of the dog. "What's your name, big fella?"

Name. The dog-puppy had to have a name.

"Champ," said Marty in a rush. "His name is Champ Hobarth. And he doesn't usually stink."

She petted the dog on the nose and smiled. "You be good, Champ Hobarth," she said. "Go home and have a bath. Make Marty fix your collar, too."

She gave Marty a length of rope with a slipknot

on the end for a leash. So he could get Champ safely home, she said. Then she turned and closed the tailgate of the truck. Marty took a last look at the wide eyes of the red dog in the cage.

"Come on, Champ," he said, and he held the giant puppy safe while the woman climbed into the truck. He watched her drive back through the lines of parked cars and then roll out onto the boulevard. On her way to the next call.

Marty wrinkled his nose against the heavy smell of fur and squinted up at the sky. The sun was no longer directly overhead. It was afternoon already and he hadn't even gotten his bike out of the rack.

If only he could think like a winner, for a minute or two, maybe he could answer the big question.

Now what, Hobarth?

# 4

# The Big Question

**M**arty squatted next to the dog and tried to think of the right thing to say. Something like: Hey, man, so what if you're a little lost? That's not a problem, it's an opportunity. Put a smile on. It's going to be a great summer.

But he didn't believe one word of it, so he gave the dog a hug instead.

From across the parking lot, he saw the Leanne girl pedaling toward him. A yellow hip pack hung from the handlebars of her bike. She stopped herself at the curb.

"He isn't your dog, is he?" she asked. "You saved his life, didn't you? That is so brave."

Marty felt his face flush. Was he supposed to answer the questions or say thank you?

The girl leaned back against the seat of her bike. "What are you going to do now?"

There it was. The big question.

"I don't know," he said. He wrapped the end of the rope leash around his hand and stood up. It felt good to tell the truth.

"You could try to find his owner. That's what I'd

25

do." She unzipped her pack and pulled out two pieces of candy. "But it could take hours. Here, want one?"

She talked so fast, all Marty could do was nod. He took one of the candies and unwrapped it and stuck it in his mouth. Spicy cinnamon juice coated his tongue.

"But then maybe he doesn't have an owner," she said. "Maybe he doesn't have a home." With one swift movement she plucked the empty wrapper out of his hand and stuffed it back into the pack.

"Everybody has a home," said Marty in between chews.

"Not necessarily, if you think about it."

He didn't want to think about it. He wound the leash tighter around his hand and wondered who she was anyway. And how could she say things like that? In front of the dog?

She adjusted the sweatband on her forehead. "I can help you. We can at least try. I'm not doing a whole lot right now."

Marty swallowed the sugary juice of the candy. It might take hours, if he had to find the dog's owner all by himself. Then when would he talk to his dad? At home in front of Francine?

"All right," he said. "You can help. I'm calling him Champ."

They divided the park, with its walking trails and pond, its picnic area and playground, in half. Then they covered it from one end to the other. But no one they spoke to had ever seen the dog Champ before. It was as if he'd been dropped from outer space.

When Leanne's watch said three o'clock, they walked together to the swimming-pool entrance. At first Marty had said, "No, not the pool." But it was getting late. What else could he do?

He kept his eyes open for David or any of the other kids from the diving team, because Leanne, who thought he was brave, had obviously missed his Olympic jump. But he didn't see anyone he knew.

A lifeguard was on duty at the front gate.

Marty explained about the dog Champ. "He has to belong to somebody," he said. "Maybe somebody in swimming."

"He's been hanging around for two days," said the lifeguard. "I think he's a stray."

Marty folded one arm protectively around the dog's neck. "Couldn't you ask over the loudspeaker anyway?"

"Please," added Leanne. She stood close on the other side of the dog. "It's life or death."

"I s'pose it wouldn't hurt. But I think you're barking up the wrong tree." The lifeguard chuckled as he turned toward the pool office.

They sat on the grass by the turnstile, waiting for a swimmer to come out and claim his dog. Leanne bought them Cokes. Marty got a cup of water for Champ, who slurped it like he hadn't had a drink for a year.

"What did you mean by life or death?" Marty asked after a while, when he decided it was better to know than to guess.

Leanne was trying to get through a clump of matted fur on the dog's back with a pink comb. "You know," she said.

Marty snapped off blades of grass and tossed them. Maybe he'd never paid a lot of attention to what happened to animals that got lost. Maybe he'd never wanted to. He looked at Leanne.

"Not everybody who goes in comes out," she said. "You know."

Maybe he had known that. Somehow. "But it's not going to happen to this guy," he said. He cupped his hand around one of Champ's front paws and tried not to think about the red dog he'd seen in the back of the Animal Control truck.

They waited a long time.

At four o'clock David pushed through the turnstile. His towel was draped around his neck like a prizefighter's.

Marty jiggled the slush in the bottom of his cup and wished he really was the incredible shrinking kid. Better yet, he wished he could vaporize David. He held on to Champ's paw as David sauntered over.

On the other side of Champ, Leanne flapped her sandal with her toes.

"It wasn't a joke, was it?" asked David when he stood in front of Marty. "Ann Louise was right. You wimped out."

"I did not."

"You always quit."

"I do not." Marty dumped the slush on the grass. Why couldn't David just shut up? "I got a cramp. I couldn't move."

"Then why didn't you try again?"

Marty stared hard at David. "Maybe I had better things to do."

David snorted. "Like what?"

Leanne's sandal made a loud *flap!* as she sat up. "Like see this dog?" she said, her voice crisp. "He was on his way to jail until Marty saved him. It was fabulous."

"Huh?"

She started to explain, but Marty said, "Never mind."

More kids came through the turnstile then. One of them called to David, and Marty watched him run to catch up.

"Honestly," grumbled Leanne. "Some people are so insensitive. Who cares if you don't know how to dive?"

Marty turned away, his face hot. She'd known all along.

"I gotta go," he said. He scrambled up, startling the dog. "Come on, Champ."

She followed him, firing questions all the way. The only one he answered was the big one.

"What are you going to do now?"

"Find the person who belongs to Champ," he said. He shifted the leash to his other hand.

"How?"

"How do you think? I'll ask people."

"Where?"

"Everywhere. I'll find his home even if it takes all summer." When had he decided this?

She hurried to keep up. "But what if he doesn't have one? Could he live with you?"

Marty shook his head no.

"Why not?"

"Lots of reasons." He bounded down the steps to the parking lot two at a time. She didn't need to know the story of his whole life, did she?

But it was the truth. There were lots of reasons the Hobarths didn't have pets. He knew them all by heart. Animals required time and the Hobarths didn't have it. They were too busy. Plus their carpet was white, their yard wasn't fenced, and the living room was always full of new sample furniture.

Plus dogs barked and cats shed and birds made gloppy messes. (No one had said much about fish.)

It had taken his appendix operation and three days in the hospital for Marty even to get Godzilla, and that was only because he'd been in pain. "Just this once, dear," his mother had said. "As long as you take care of him all by yourself."

Nobody had noticed the tree frogs yet.

When Marty reached the bike rack, Leanne held the leash while he pulled his bike out from the slot. She bent down and gave Champ a kiss on the head.

"He does need a bath, Marty," she said. "I'd keep him if I could, but I can't. I'm staying with my aunt in an apartment and they don't allow pets."

She wrote her name and telephone number on a tablet she kept in her pack and gave it to him. She watched while he stuffed it in his pocket. Then she asked him for his. In case she found a lead, she said.

Reluctantly he gave it to her.

"We'll talk!" she said in a whirl.

And before he could tell her to forget it, before he could say that he and Champ could take care of things just fine by themselves, she was gone. Yellow pack bouncing, ponytail flying.

A girl tornado.

He turned back to the dog. "Don't worry, Champ. We won't need her."

Champ pranced at the end of the leash. Marty wound the end of it around his right hand and swung one leg over the center bar of his bike. He'd never had to walk a dog and ride a bike at the same time before. He'd have to go slow.

And he'd have to go home.

Because not only was it too late to bike down to his dad's furniture store, but what would he do with the dog once he got there? Take him inside and let him sit on a sofa? Hardly.

He gripped the handlebars and gave a wobbly push off.

As soon as his dad got home from the store, he,

Marty, would tell him everything. He'd start with the dog and work into the dive.

"Dad! Guess what!" He practiced as he pedaled jerkily across the parking lot. "Remember the dog who tried to eat your sunglasses?"

It sounded sort of funny. His dad would laugh. It would be a good place to start.

# 5

# Mr. Chu's Cookies

**M**arty held the garden hose over Champ's back and watched the water gush out. Suds from the shampoo he'd found in the upstairs bathroom slid down Champ's wet fur and plopped onto the growing mountain of foam on the grass.

It was the second washing.

"Yuck," said Francine from a distance. "He's still dirty."

Marty smiled to himself. Things were already going better than he'd expected. Bringing Champ home had made his sister forget all about his diving tryout.

He leaned over the rope leash, which was tied to a leg of the picnic table, and carefully rinsed the fur below Champ's ears. "Good dog," he said. "Very good dog."

Champ looked up, his eyes darting nervously to the hose.

Francine took a step closer. "He's so big. Are you sure he's a dog?"

"I'm sure." Marty moved the hose along Champ's spine. He wondered what would she say if she knew Champ was still a puppy.

"Well, he's not coming in the house even if he does get clean. Why'd you bring him here anyway? Dad will be furious."

Marty held the hose over Champ's hips. Water spilled down the feathering of his tail and made it look like fringe. "Almost done, Champ," Marty said. "Then we'll dry you off."

"That's another thing, Marty." Francine was now on the other side of the picnic table. "He doesn't look like a champion anything. I bet his real name is Mister Dirt." She laughed. "Get it? The opposite of Mister Clean?"

Marty rolled his eyes. "Don't you have something to do? Like study for your dumb class?"

"Enriched Language Arts is hardly a dumb class, Marty." Francine's eyes flashed. "It's for gifted students. But you wouldn't understand about that."

Of course not. He was ungifted. How could he forget?

"Then don't you have someplace to go?"

"Yeah, but not yet. I'm baby-sitting. Hey, I almost forgot. Did you get on the team?"

At just that moment the hose accidentally slipped in Marty's hand. It swerved like a snake toward Francine, spraying water up over the picnic table and making a rainbow in the late-afternoon sunlight.

"*Marty!*" Francine jumped back. Her shirt was soaked. "I'm telling!" She spun around and ran toward the house.

Marty twisted the nozzle on the hose until it shut off the water flow. Then he reached for his beach towel.

"Don't worry about her," he said to the dripping Champ. "She's just jealous she didn't find you first. Everything's going to be fine."

And it would be. Because he'd planned it all out, on the ride home, every part of it.

This time his dad would listen for sure.

Why, when he heard the part about how Marty'd saved the dog, he'd probably tell Marty that he would have done the same thing himself. He'd like Champ now that he was clean. He'd want to pet him. He'd say, "Hi there, big fella. Welcome to the Hobarths'."

As Marty rubbed Champ's back with the towel, he pictured Champ and his dad sitting together, being friends. He imagined his dad inviting Champ to stay as long as he wanted. Maybe even forever.

He fluffed the fur of Champ's neck, his fingers tingling with hope. "How would you like to live here with me?" he said. "If we can't find your home, that is."

Champ licked Marty's ear. Then, without warning, he shook. Water spattered Marty's face and shoulders as the shake moved down Champ's body from his head to the tip of his tail.

"Don't *do* stuff like that, Champ!" Marty thought of his mother's white carpeting. And the glass angels on the coffee table. "Unless you're in my room."

He found a dry corner of the towel and wiped it across his face and arms. Then he gave Champ's head a last buff. The odor of swamp lingered, but it was lots fainter now. Maybe after dinner he'd bike to the pet store in the shopping mall and buy some real dog soap. Something potent, like anti-skunk shampoo. But in the meantime . . .

"I know," he said, and he dropped the towel on the grass.

He left Champ tied to the picnic table and raced into the house. He grabbed the bottle of perfume he'd given his mother for her birthday and ran back outside. He pressed the pump squirter twice.

*Pfft, pfft.*

The musky scent of Glorious Nights perfume filled the air. Marty gave Champ a reassuring pat on the head. "Everything's going to be fine," he said. "You'll see."

Of course his dad was going to be disappointed when he heard the part about the dive. But Marty was sure he'd understand, once he knew the whole story. Plus with a new dog to take care of, who'd have time to be on a team anyway?

Marty gave the perfume one more squirt.

Champ sneezed.

And at the same moment the Hobarth's F & A van rolled into the driveway.

Marty's dad was home.

Marty ignored the fluttering in his stomach and stood up. He untied the leash from the leg of the picnic table and wound the end around his hand. "Here we go, guy," he said to Champ. "Be polite." Then he spread a huge smile across his face and waited for his dad to climb out of the van.

But his dad didn't. Instead he sat behind the wheel like a statue, his eyes fixed on the dog.

Marty waved.

Finally Mr. Hobarth shut off the engine. He opened the door and, in slow motion, stepped out. In his hands were two white cartons with wire handles, and a bag.

Takeout food. He'd stopped at Foo Chu Express, Marty's favorite. It was a good sign.

Marty watched him walk across the lawn. "Dad!" he hollered. "Guess what!"

Heavily Mr. Hobarth sat down on the bench. He placed the cartons and the bag on the table. He looked at Marty. Then he looked at Champ.

"Marty," he said.

Marty kept the smile on his face even though his arm felt almost out of joint from Champ's straining against the leash. "Remember the dog who tried to eat your sunglasses, Dad? This is him."

"I can see that."

"Only he's clean now. He looks good, don't you think? I gave him a bath. No, actually I gave him two baths." Marty managed to get Champ to sit by standing over him like a rodeo rider.

"Why is he here, Marty?"

Marty tried to remember what he'd planned to say

first, but the look on his dad's face made him forget. He went right to the important part. "He's lost. He needs me."

"You know our rule on pets, Marty."

His dad was not supposed to be thinking about that now.

Marty made his smile wider. "But this is different, Dad. It's an emergency. The Animal Control officer was going to take him. Somebody complained. He was on his way to jail." The words rushed out in a jumble. "I had to do something."

Mr. Hobarth sighed.

"Don't you think he's nice, Dad?"

"It doesn't matter if I think he's nice. He's a stray. He's a health hazard."

Marty's fingers had gone numb from gripping the rope leash. He rubbed them against his jeans. "A what?"

"Use your head, Marty. He could be diseased. Or vicious. You don't know anything about him."

Marty tried hard to keep up the smile. "Yes, I do. He's friendly and clean and he likes bologna sandwiches. He hasn't bitten me once."

"You shouldn't have brought him here."

"But, Dad." Marty whispered, for emphasis. "He might be *homeless.*"

Mr. Hobarth pressed his fingers against his temples as if the discussion was giving him a headache. "Marty," he said. "I was the one who called in the complaint."

Marty's breath caught. "You?"

"He needs to be taken off the street. It's for his own good. And it's not jail, it's the city animal shelter." Mr. Hobarth looked at his watch. "I'll take him there now, before I drop Francine at the Smiths. I have a downtown-merchants' meeting in an hour. Can you heat up your own dinner?"

Dinner? Who cared about dinner?

"We don't have to keep him, Dad. I'll find his home tonight. Just give me tonight. I'll start looking right now."

Mr. Hobarth stood. "I'm sorry, Marty."

Marty wrapped one arm around Champ's neck and looked up at his dad. "If Mom was here, she'd say yes. She says we're supposed to *help* the homeless."

His father frowned. "That's not fair, Marty, and you know it. We're not talking about people here."

"But not everybody who goes in comes out of that place, Dad. Maybe you didn't know that."

Mr. Hobarth put his hand on Marty's shoulder. It pressed like a lead weight. "I'm as sorry as you are, son, but he's not our problem. You should have let the Animal Control officer take him. You should have thought this through."

"Dad. Please."

"No."

As Mr. Hobarth walked toward the house, Marty bent over and buried his face in the curve of Champ's huge shoulder.

He *had* thought this through, every part of it. Even down to where Champ would sleep (his bedroom rug) and eat (the back porch). It could have worked. It would have worked. How could his dad be so mean?

He nuzzled Champ's fur until the oil in the Glorious Nights perfume made his eyes sting and he had to stand up to dry them.

If only he'd explained it better. If only he'd remembered the speech like he'd planned it.

But he hadn't.

Once again he'd messed up. He couldn't even do a rescue right.

Champ pulled away. His nose, pointed at the Foo Chu cartons, quivered.

"How can you think of food now?" Marty asked.

Champ inched toward the table.

"All right." Marty stepped around Champ and reached for the bag. He opened it and saw that Mr. Chu had sent along three fortune cookies. Marty took one out.

He broke it and removed the fortune so the dog wouldn't swallow it. "Here," he said. He dropped the broken cookie in the grass.

While Champ crunched, Marty unfolded the small strip of paper. It read:

*Invest in kindness and your reward will be great.*

That was a joke.

Helping Champ had been kind, but it hadn't gotten him a reward. It had gotten him into trouble.

He dropped the fortune on the grass and pulled out another cookie.

The fortune read:

*Hope can change the world.*

Marty squeezed the paper into a little ball. Who cared about changing the world at a time like this? Why didn't Mr. Chu's fortunes ever tell you how to do the important stuff?

Champ nosed him for more food, so he took the last crimped, half-moon cookie out of the bag.

The fortune said:

*Now is the time to follow your heart.*

Marty knelt down on the grass. This one he'd seen before. This one he understood.

His mother had told him that's what she was doing when she decided to go back to college to learn how to be an archeologist. She was following her heart. She'd said it meant doing what she believed was right even though not everybody agreed.

She'd even written it in big letters on the family activities calendar so they'd all remember it when things got hard. When she had to study all the time and write papers and leave early in the morning before he went to school. (He had to make his own lunches!)

Follow your heart. Now is the time.

The words echoed inside Marty's head. But what if a person couldn't follow his heart? What if he wanted to, but somebody wouldn't let him? Then what?

He smoothed the small paper back and forth

against his cheek. What if somebody had told his mother she couldn't go back to college? Would she have given up?

Just then the back screen door slammed. Marty turned. His dad and Francine were coming down the back steps.

Quickly he scooped up the fortunes and stuffed them into his pocket. He looked at Champ, sprawled next to him, licking cookie crumbs out of the grass.

Could he, Marty Hobarth, just forget him? And maybe let him die?

He laid his hand on Champ's neck. Underneath the still-damp fur, he could feel the dog's pulse, calm and steady.

If his dad had asked anything else, he'd go along, like he always did, even if he didn't want to. But not this time. Not when a life was at stake. This time, if he went along, he'd be the biggest zilch on Earth. This time the answer had to be no.

He stood. "Dad," he said.

But Mr. Hobarth held up his hand to stop him. "There's nothing more to say, Marty. We've got to go."

"I told him, Dad," Francine interrupted. Her face was smug, her shirt dry. "I said it was stupid to bring a dog here."

"Francey." Mr. Hobarth looked stern. "It wasn't stupid. It was a lesson learned. That's all."

Marty's shoulders sagged. His dad wasn't going to listen to him now no matter what. Not about the dog, not about the dive, not about anything. Not when he thought he was teaching Marty something.

Marty knelt in front of Champ and beamed him a silent message. *I'm not quitting on you, Champ. I'm going to help. I don't know how yet, but I will. So hang on.*

The dog stared back, his gaze unwavering.

He'd gotten the message, Marty was sure. And so he kept it up, beaming the same promise over and over, as he opened the van's back door for Champ, and as he watched Champ's face take up almost the whole window as the van rolled down the street. *I'll be there. Hang on.*

When the van disappeared around the curve of Fox Lane, Marty ran for the house. He sprinted up the back steps and gave the screen door a powerful yank. In the kitchen he reached into his pocket and pulled out the papers. He set the fortunes aside and unfolded the note from the girl tornado.

*Leanne P. Igler,* it said above the phone number. *Call me anytime.*

He grabbed the telephone and dialed. Because for starters, he didn't even know where the jail was. Or what, exactly, he would do when he got there. He was going to need all the help he could get. And it wasn't the time to be picky.

# 6

# Incognito

**L**eanne Igler was fast. She knocked at the Hobarths' back door, ready to help, only minutes after Marty's phone call. Marty got up from the kitchen chair. He was chewing the last forkful of moo goo gai pan. He'd warmed it up after all, because deciding to follow your heart, he found, made you hungry.

He swallowed and invited her in.

She said she was sorry about Champ.

He said he was too.

She glanced around the kitchen. "Since I'm not doing a whole lot tonight, I thought I'd show you the map. So you know where we're going tomorrow."

She wasn't doing a whole lot tomorrow, either, she'd told him on the phone, and so she'd offered to go along.

He was glad.

She looked at the family activities calendar on the refrigerator. "This is nice," she said. "I bet you have a fun family."

Marty collected his dishes and set them in the

sink with a clatter. He'd never thought of his family as fun. Especially not now.

He turned on the faucet while Leanne wandered out to the hall.

"What's all this?" she asked.

Marty peered out from the doorway and groaned. She'd found the awards cabinet.

"Just stuff," he answered. "Where's the map?"

She ignored his question. With two hands she lifted a polished cup off the shelf. "Wow," she said.

"My dad won a race. He almost got in the Olympics. It was a long time ago."

Carefully she slid the trophy back onto the shelf. "Who's this?"

He had to walk out into the hall in order to see what she was looking at. It was the picture of his mother in her graduation cap and gown. "That was when my mom went back to college. She's an archeologist now."

"Wow," said Leanne again. "Has she found any tombs or anything?"

Marty shook his head no. "She's on her first dig right now. In Mexico."

Leanne touched the wood frame of his mother's picture. "She's coming back though. Right?"

What kind of goofy question was that? "Sure, she's coming back. She's a mom."

Leanne started to say something but instead turned back to the cabinet. She moved her fingers across the collection of hanging ribbons.

"My sister wins spelling contests," he said, because he knew she'd ask. "Now can I see the map?"

"But where are your things, Marty?"

Marty tapped his fingers against the door frame. "I don't like to show off," he said.

It wasn't a total lie. He did have a few awards. One for perfect attendance at school two years in a row, and one for helping in the Red Cross blood drive. Plus little plastic participation trophies for school sports, which everybody got no matter how they played.

He turned and went back into the kitchen.

Behind him Leanne was still talking. "I like seeing where people live. It tells you a lot, you know? It gives you a sense."

Sure, he knew. Like what's a zilch who can't dive doing in a family like this?

He ran hot water over his plate. "Let's get started," he said. "Before my dad gets home."

She insisted on seeing his room first. And holding Godzilla, who turned a chalky brown from the noise of a strange voice. "Wait until he calms down," Marty said. "Then I'll take him out."

She stared up at his model of the solar system. Her favorite planet, she said, was Jupiter. (He'd never met anybody who had a favorite planet.) She'd had a cat named Jupiter, in Kansas.

Marty folded his arms across his chest. "The map?"

She knelt down, opened her pack, and spread the map on the floor.

It was hard to read, what with all the pencil marks, the arrows, the colored circles. The margins were crowded with scribbles that looked like code.

"Geez," said Marty. "What happened to this?"

She smiled. "Me."

The good news was, Leanne Igler had been exploring Johnson Falls on her rented bicycle ever since she'd arrived on the train from Pittsburgh to visit her Aunt Jen for the summer.

"Pittsburgh?" Marty asked.

"That's where we live, me and my dad."

"I thought it was Kansas."

"Kansas was before Pittsburgh," she said, impatient. "I thought you wanted to look at the map."

"Right."

She'd seen about everything, she said, pointing to different Xs on the map. She'd been about everywhere. Including the Wirth Granite factory (they made cemetery headstones) and the greenhouses of Falls Floral (they'd given her a free rose) and the Walking Billboards advertising agency, which could put anything you wanted on the front of a T-shirt.

They were places Marty'd never even heard of.

She smoothed her hand over a crease in the map. "It's a nice little city. I like the way the streets are named after presidents."

Marty blinked. They were? Since when?

"I didn't see the animal jail, Marty. But I know where it is." She pressed one pink fingernail against the top edge of the map. "Here."

Marty sat down. He stared at the intersecting lines

and the tiny block letters that showed the corner of Van Buren Street and Thirty-third Avenue. He swallowed a bump in his throat.

Champ was right there, right now. In a cell, drinking out of a tin cup, waiting for him. Marty closed his eyes and beamed him a long-distance message.

*Hang on, buddy. We're coming.*

Leanne rested her elbows on her knees. "Got any ideas about what we'll do once we get there?"

"Not yet," said Marty. "But something will turn up." It had to. Because, he guessed, that's how it must work when you followed your heart. You knew just the next thing to do, one thing at a time.

Leanne pushed her hair back away from her eyes. "We might have to steal him, you know."

He knew.

"And hide him someplace until we find his home."

Marty drummed his fingers on the map. "Unless something turns up." Like maybe his dad would change his mind.

"We better go incognito," said Leanne.

"Incognito?"

"In disguise. In case we have to do something illegal."

Marty swallowed. He'd never done anything illegal . . . at least that he knew of. He'd never been incognito, either. Except on Halloween.

"Can I see the lizard now?"

"I guess." Marty leaned over the terrarium and lifted Godzilla out. Gently he set him on the floor.

"Zill," he said. "Meet Leanne."

The chameleon bobbed his head, and then began to wiggle-walk across the map of Johnson Falls. He stomped over Lincoln, Madison, and Polk avenues like the real Godzilla and—oh no!—he crushed the river bridge. He stepped on the squares that marked the college campus, obliterating tile-roofed buildings and the football stadium and the statue of the frontier general Josiah Johnson. He knocked out power lines and streetlights and scraped a wing off the hospital until he finally, mercifully, stopped on the corner of Van Buren and Thirty-third, his tail speckled green and switching.

It was a long trip.

"Wow," said Leanne. She pointed to Godzilla's toe. "We'll be exactly right there tomorrow morning. Incognito and ready for anything."

Marty looked up at the planets of his mini solar system. They swung in the breeze from his open window, Earth dangling perilously close to the sun. He crossed his fingers behind his back, took a deep breath, and hoped something legal would turn up.

# 7

# Jail

**G**etting out of the house the next morning was easier than Marty had thought. He overslept. By the time he got down to the kitchen, the only thing waiting for him was messages on the "Keep in Touch" chalkboard by the phone.

His dad and Francine had left notes saying where they'd be and when. His dad downtown to the F & A, Francine to her class for gifted superbrains.

A smiley face had been drawn at the bottom of the board as usual.

They were pretending that nothing was wrong. Like they hadn't just put a dog in jail. Like Champ had never happened.

Well, he could play that game too.

He'd done it last night when his dad had come home from his meeting, pretending to be asleep so he wouldn't have to listen to another lecture on thinking things through.

He picked up the chalk and wrote: *Real busy all day. Home for dinner.*

He was glad now that he hadn't told them what had happened at the pool. They'd figure he was spending the day with the diving team, no questions asked. He drew nose plugs on the smiley face and a wavy line that made the face look like it was half underwater. Then he went to the cupboard.

He poured some Frosted Flakes out of the cereal box and dumped them into a small plastic bag so he could eat while he biked. Then he dialed Leanne's number.

"Ready?" he asked when she answered.

"Ready."

They met in front of the Jiffy Mart. Marty almost didn't recognize her, with her aviator sunglasses and the oversized baseball hat that hid her ponytail. She didn't smile when he brought his bike to a stop next to hers. But then maybe she didn't recognize him either.

He pushed the mirrored sunglasses, which he'd found in the kitchen junk drawer, up against his nose. Then he rolled the sleeves of his dad's old fishing shirt up to his elbows. "It's me," he said. "Incognito."

"Hi," she said.

He scooped some Frosted Flakes out of the bag and popped them into his mouth. He wished now he'd gotten up a little earlier, so he could have put them in a bowl with milk. Already he was thirsty and they hadn't even started. He forced a dry swallow. "We'll have to cross the river bridge."

"I know," she said, her voice as solemn as her face.

But then it isn't every day you set out to save a life.

They skirted the downtown business district so Marty wouldn't get too close to his dad's furniture store, and then they headed north. The farther they went, the less Marty recognized. Although Leanne seemed to know where she was, he rarely came this far, and never on his bike.

What had he been doing all his life? Hiding?

They began to pedal the slow rise to the Mississippi River bridge. When the hill steepened, they got off their bikes and walked them. Already Marty could hear the noise of the trucks and cars, their tires whining as they sped across the bridge.

He leaned into the handlebars to keep his bike (and himself) moving up the hill. Ahead, the bridge loomed. Good thing his mother didn't know he was this far from home.

They crossed the bridge single file on a narrow iron walkway. Traffic rushed past them, making wind gusts that swept at Marty's face and once almost knocked Leanne's baseball cap off. Below, a barge gave a foggy blast of its horn.

The bridge was at least two blocks long.

When they were safely on the other side, they stopped for a map check. Then they pushed off, once again heading north. They passed a factory, the air smelling like burnt marshmallows. The city bus garage came next, and then a dump.

Just when Marty figured they'd never get there,

they did. They stood on the corner of Van Buren and Thirty-third, straddling their bikes.

Leanne took her hat off and untwisted her pony-tail. "Well," she said. "Finally."

Marty looked across the street. Animal jail was cement gray, and small. It sat back from the road, off by itself, squares of chain-link fencing jutting out from the sides.

And there was barking.

A sign in the front yard said MID-STATE ANIMAL SHELTER (his dad had been right about that, any-way). It had a picture on it too. A bunch of animals sitting under a bright red umbrella. As if they were trying to keep dry in a storm.

Leanne shoved the baseball cap back on her head. "It says shelter but it means jail. Every city has one. They're all the same. I hope we don't have to steal Champ. It could get tricky."

A wave of panic rolled through Marty's stomach. What if they did have to steal Champ, and they got caught? What if the Animal Control officer he'd met at the pool (and lied to) was in there? She'd prob-ably recognize him, even incognito. Somebody would call his dad. He hadn't thought of that. That would be horrible.

He balanced his bike with one hand and rubbed his stomach with the other. The Frosted Flakes he'd eaten felt like gravel sitting right above his belt.

He almost wished he'd never gotten himself into this. He almost wished he was at the swimming pool, trying the dive over again, instead of being way up here, on the edge of the map, about to steal a dog.

Quitting would be understandable at a time like this. Maybe he'd misunderstood the cookie. Maybe you were only supposed to follow your heart if you were a grown-up.

But Champ was waiting for him. And Leanne, he saw, was already pedaling up the drive.

He straightened his sunglasses, took a deep breath, and followed.

There were several cars in the parking lot, and a bike rack that was half full. Marty pushed his front wheel into an empty slot next to Leanne's. Then he bent down and pulled a pebble out of his shoe. He dusted off his jeans. He unbuttoned the neck of the fishing shirt. When he began rerolling both sleeves, one at a time, Leanne said, "Can we go in now?"

Marty supposed they'd have to.

They crossed the parking lot, pulled open the front door, and walked in.

The lobby was dim. Marty saw a group of kids in one corner watching a video on how to hold a puppy. Near them a boy in a green vest unfolded newspapers at a table. A girl, also in green, was mopping the floor. Marty and Leanne stepped out of her way.

In front of the window was a cage of kittens.

"Oh!" said Leanne. "Look!"

An orange kitten stuck a paw out and mewed at her. "Adopt ME!" said a card hooked to the top of the cage.

"Isn't it cute?"

Marty nodded. He turned a slow circle, scanning the rest of the room.

Aha.

Behind the counter was the office. In the office was a man with a lot of curly hair. He was not the Animal Control officer. He was not even in uniform. He was on the phone. He smiled at Marty.

Marty tried to smile back. Like hi. What a fun place.

Past the office, Marty saw another door. THIS WAY TO VIEW ANIMALS, a sign said.

Marty fidgeted with his sunglasses. Could they just walk in? Or were they supposed to wait for the man at the desk?

Just then more people came in. They crowded around the counter, in front of the man. Leanne was cooing over the orange kitten. Marty pulled her by the wrist. "Come on!"

They went through the back door into a hallway. It was big. It smelled like a laundry room, and it had lots more doors.

Which way was Champ?

They split up. Marty turned right and followed barking to a room that was long and narrow, lined with chain-link doors.

It was a row of kennels, and in them, a row of

dogs. Sixteen to be exact, Marty counted. But not one of them was Champ.

There were big dogs and small dogs, fuzzy ones and smooth-coated ones. Some had long, sweepy tails, others had only stubs. In one kennel a black dog nursed her puppies.

As Marty walked down the row, the dogs stuck their noses through the fenced doors. Tails wagged. Eyes peered up. Barking echoed off the cement walls.

And Marty felt sick.

Fastened to each door was a white "Adopt ME!" card, and on each card was the date the dog had arrived and the reason why the dog was there. *Family moving. Won't hunt. Can't train. Stray.*

They were throwaway dogs, every last one. Marty wished he could steal them all.

"Marty!" It was Leanne. "I found him!"

Marty forced himself to turn away from the peering eyes. He followed Leanne into another room, also lined with kennels.

In the second stall stood Champ, on his hind legs, his front paws pushed through the wire fencing of his door.

Marty rushed up. The familiar scent of Glorious Nights perfume filled his head. He reached in. "Champ," he said. "Here I am."

The dog stamped so furiously that one foot caught the edge of his water pail and dumped it. Water spilled across the kennel floor and out to Marty's shoes.

"Are you looking for a pet?"

Both Marty and Leanne spun around. It was the man with the curly hair.

"Um," said Marty.

"Yes, possibly," said Leanne.

The man smiled. "This one's a stray. He's big, isn't he? A Bernard cross, I'm sure."

"We love dogs," said Leanne.

"Especially Bernard crosses," said Marty.

"Two dogs came in yesterday," said the man, and he pointed to the next stall.

Marty looked over Leanne's shoulder. It was the red dog. The one he'd seen in the rescue truck.

"They'll be staying with us for while," said the man. He reached through the fenced door and patted Champ's head. "They can't be adopted yet."

"They can't?" asked Marty and Leanne, at the same time.

The man shook his head no. "State law. We observe strays for five full business days. Our veterinarian has to check them too."

Marty counted on his fingers. Five full business days, plus the two weekend days, meant the middle of the next week!

He could find Champ's home by then easy. (Or get his dad to change his mind!) Why, he could probably find homes for the other dogs too. Maybe even the mother dog and her puppies. Then nobody would have to steal anybody.

"Don't owners ever come in and claim them?" asked Leanne.

"Not very often," said the man. He called over his shoulder for someone to get the mop, and then he began to walk away. "Stop by and see us again," he said on his way out.

Leanne followed him. "To the cats," she said.

Marty looked down the row of kennels. Then he stepped up to Champ's door and smoothed his hand over Champ's sticking-out paw. He didn't want to stop by and see them again. He wanted to stay. He wanted to climb into every stall and sit with every dog. He wanted to pet them and tell them everything would be fine now that he was there.

If only there was a way.

The girl from the lobby appeared then, pushing a large mop bucket on wheels. Up close, Marty saw the word VOLUNTEER written across the front pocket of her green vest.

Volunteer? Could anybody do that?

Marty asked her.

"Oh man, yes," she said, huffing as she sloshed the stringy mop across the floor. "We need lots more help here. Applications are at the counter."

Marty turned to Champ. "Be right back," he said, and he bolted for the lobby.

He was at the counter outside the office in an instant. He lifted an application off the stack. He stared down at it, almost unbelieving.

BE A WINNER! it said in large boldface type. HELP THE ANIMALS THIS SUMMER!

Marty steadied himself against the counter as he read the words again, because if he didn't, he thought he might faint.

The cookie had been right. *He* had been right. It really *worked* to follow your heart, one step at a time. And this was what he was supposed to do next.

"Marty." Leanne had come up behind him. "What's that?"

He handed her the application. "The something," he said. "It turned up."

While she read, he pulled off his sunglasses. The room, he saw, wasn't dim at all. It was bright and cheery, summer sunlight streaming in the windows.

"Are you gonna do this?" Leanne sounded worried.

"Sure I am," he answered, and it was the truth. He'd never been so sure of anything in his life. He was going to help the animals. Not just Champ, but all of them.

He was going to be a winner.

# 8

# Super Double-Top Extra Cheese

**I**t was easy for Marty to say yes to the man at the shelter when he asked, "Any chance you two might want to be volunteers?"

And it was easy for him to say "See you tomorrow!" when he and Leanne finally left, after he'd marched through both kennel rooms whispering promises to each and every dog.

The hard part was figuring out how, exactly, he was going to pull it off. Especially since he was supposed to be at the pool every day, diving.

And then there was Leanne, who all of a sudden had turned chicken.

"Come on," said Marty as they glided down Johnson Boulevard toward the Dairy Queen on their bikes. "Volunteering will be fun. You'll like it."

"I don't know, Marty."

"Where'd you get that jail idea anyway? The place was nice."

Leanne, lagging behind, didn't answer.

Marty tried again. "You didn't see anybody dead, did you?"

"Well, no."

"Well, okay then." He turned into the Dairy Queen and brought his bike to a stop on the matted lawn. "Don't you want to help Champ?" he asked. "And the cats?"

Leanne rolled up next to him. "Of course I do."

"Then what's the big deal?"

She climbed off her bike and tilted it against a picnic table. "All right, Marty," she sighed. "I'll try it. Unless something terrible happens."

What a worrywart.

Marty rummaged through one pocket for his money. He almost told her about the fortune cookie then. About how terrible things couldn't happen when you followed your heart. But he didn't. Because what if the fortune, like a birthday-cake wish, worked only if you kept it secret?

They sat under a tree, sipping root-beer floats, as they examined the volunteer applications Marty'd taken from the shelter. On the bottom of the page was a place for a parent or guardian's signature.

It was not a good start.

Marty tapped the paper with the tip of his spoon. "No way will my dad sign this," he said. "He'd be mad if he even knew I was there today."

Leanne looked hopeful. "Then maybe you shouldn't do it."

"I have to do it."

"Why?"

It was hard not to mention the cookie. "I just do."

Leanne scooped a mound of the creamy soft-serve

onto her spoon. "I think you should try to talk to your dad again. Explain it better. That's what I'd do."

Marty closed his mouth around the straw and took a long pull of the cold root beer. He imagined what would happen if he told his dad he didn't have time to go diving because he had to bike across the Mississippi River bridge every morning so he could take care of throwaway dogs. It sent a chill from the roof of his mouth to his toes. He shook his head no.

"Aunt Jen will sign mine," said Leanne. "She'll be glad I found something to do when she's at work. She was worried I might get bored. Too bad she can't sign yours."

It gave him an idea.

"What if she could?" he said. "Without knowing it, I mean. What if, after she signs yours, you wrote my name on it too? We could pretend I'm your brother."

"Marty Igler," said Leanne. "Visiting from Pittsburgh." She leaned back against the tree, and Marty could almost hear her thinking it over.

He scraped a spoonful of foamy root beer from the edge of his cup while he waited for her to decide. Ordinarily he wouldn't suggest something like that. It was dishonest. But what else could he do? Desert Champ and the other dogs just because his dad wouldn't sign some piece of paper?

"Okay, Marty." Leanne sat up. She was looking perky again. "Maybe this will be sort of fun."

"It will be. I promise."

She began, then, describing the cats she'd seen. One the color of chocolate chips. Another like orange marmalade. "I could hug them all day," she said. "Poor things. I wish people in Aunt Jen's apartment building could have pets."

Marty took the last sip of his root beer and stood up. If only he could change his dad's mind as easily as he'd changed Leanne's. If only the rest of what he had to do, before he could bike down to the shelter the next morning and start volunteering, would turn out like this!

He spent the evening catching crickets. It gave him an excuse to stay away from his dad, who was watching the Minnesota Twins on televsion, and Francine, who thought bugs were disgusting.

Besides. Godzilla and the tree frogs did need to eat.

And he, Marty, needed to get ready to deliver the first really serious lie of his life. He'd worked on it most of the afternoon, which was no big surprise, because as lies went, it had to be better than good.

It had to be perfect.

Not only one hundred percent believable, but able to stretch out over weeks. Maybe even the whole summer. As long as he needed it. As long as it took to find homes for all those dogs.

He'd rehearsed it in front of his mirror until he could almost say it backward. But now, crawling around under the porch with his bug net and jar, just the thought of it made him sweat.

If lies came in sizes like pizzas—small, medium, and large—this one would be a super double-top extra cheese.

He was under the steps, hovering over a cricket, when the screen door slammed and he heard his dad's footsteps above him. He made a quick swipe with the bug net, but his timing was off and the cricket bounced out of range.

"Marty? Where are you?"

"Under here, Dad."

His dad leaned over the railing. "Any luck?"

"Only three, plus flies." Marty knelt in place, pebbles denting his knees. Maybe he could just stay there, under the steps, when he told his dad.

"How was practice today, Mart?"

"Good. Everything went real good."

"Good."

"Yup, real good."

"I bet you worked hard."

For a split second Marty flashed to the long bike ride. "Yeah," he answered. "But, um, Dad . . ."

"Marty, come up here. I've hardly seen you since I got home."

Shoot.

Marty blew a cobweb away from his face as he crawled over the stones. When he reached the edge of the overhang, he stood and set his things between the spindles of the railing. He watched the flies he'd caught ricochet off the sides of the glass jar in a panic. He knew just how they felt. He took a deep breath and started in. "Dad," he said. "I'm supposed to give you a message for parents and guardians."

"And what's that?"

"It's from our coach. He said you're not supposed to ask us questions right now or visit the pool. He said you're supposed to let us be by ourselves. He's teaching us how to think like winners."

"Ah," said his dad.

Marty glanced up quickly, to see if it was working. It was. So he focused again on the frantic flies. "Is that okay with you, Dad?"

"It certainly is, son. It's very okay."

Marty could tell without even looking that his dad's smile had grown. It made his knees go loose. He wrapped one hand around a spindle of the railing and held on tight because he didn't know how long he could stand there acting ho-hum, as if he were telling the truth. Just when he thought he'd cave in, the sound of cheering erupted from the television in the living room.

"Must be a hit, Dad," he said, almost afraid to hope. "Were the Twins batting?"

"Yes!" His dad turned and charged into the house. The screen door banged shut after him. "A triple!" he shouted. "It's about time!"

Marty sagged against the railing and groaned.

It was not a fun thing, lying to your dad. Not a

fun thing at all. Maybe he should have tried to explain it better, like Leanne had suggested. Maybe he should have told the truth.

But what if his dad had said no?

He turned his back to the cheering from the television and forced himself to think of Champ. Champ in his kennel, at the shelter. Champ, who would pace with worry if his friend Marty never came back for him. His friend Marty, who had decided to tell his dad the truth and was now spending the rest of his life on a diving board.

Marty gripped the edge of the overhang. He couldn't desert Champ. He wouldn't!

Besides, when this was all over, his dad would be plenty proud of him. He wouldn't even care about the lies.

The shelter probably gave prizes to their volunteers, for being winners with the animals. Ribbons or something. Or maybe even trophies. They'd give him one. He'd lug it home and show it to his dad. He'd say, "Look, Dad." His dad would say, "Wow, son."

Marty took a big breath of the warm night air and felt the power begin to flow back into his arms and his legs. He stepped away from the railing and brushed the pebble dust from his knees.

He closed his eyes and beamed a long-distance message to the jail. "Stop pacing, Champ," he whispered. "Everything's going to be okay. Very okay."

# 9

# The Family

**T**he bike ride to the Mid-State Animal Shelter the next morning didn't seem nearly as difficult as it had been the day before.

Once Marty left his house and his street behind him, the bad dream he'd had (Stop, please! I'll tell the truth! Just don't make me dive or I'll drown!) began to fade. The farther he biked, the more his excitement at the day ahead began to grow.

At the corner of Johnson Boulevard, the stand of white pines made the air smell tangy and fresh. Marty stuck one arm out and let a clump of the soft needles brush against his fingers as he pedaled by.

It was going to be a great day. Noteworthy, as his mother would say. The kind of day a guy only runs into every once in a while, and so he remembers it. A day like the last day of school, when his teacher, Ms. Dixon, had surprised the class with a visit from her cousin the magician. While the other classes had sorted books and cleaned desks, Marty and his classmates had spent the day making quarters disappear up sleeves and poking around in the sword box and feeding carrots to the rabbit that came with the hat.

Yes, it was going to be that kind of day.

And he was going to spend it being somebody else. Somebody by the name of Igler, from Pittsburgh. Somebody trusted by dogs and admired by people and indispensable to everybody. He could hardly wait.

He met Leanne in front of the Jiffy Mart. "Did you bring it?" he asked.

"Hi to you, too," she said. She pulled the volunteer application out of her yellow pack and handed it to him.

He looked down at it. "Leanne P. Igler," it said in tidy, even lettering on the first line. After it, wedged in the remaining space to the margin, was added, "and her brother Marty Igler." Underneath, Leanne had written, "Visiting from Pittsburgh for the summer." On the next line was the address of Leanne's aunt's apartment: 4818 Heights Drive, #319, and then the telephone number. At the bottom, where it said "Parent or guardian," Marty saw the slanting signature of Leanne's aunt: Jennifer P. Igler.

Leanne pointed to it. "The P stands for Patrice. Same as mine."

Marty nodded absently as he read over the application again. It felt strange to see your name faked like that and your address wrong and some other grown-up's name on the line, giving you permission. He handed the paper back to Leanne.

"Aunt Jen said it's an honor, being a volunteer. We should be proud, Marty."

Marty wrapped his fingers around both hand grips and squeezed. He ought to remember that instead of thinking about the lies.

He watched her refold the paper and stick it back in her pack. Before she zipped it shut, she dug out two pieces of Bubblicious and gave him one. Then they pushed off in the direction of the shelter.

This time they didn't need a map. They pedaled an easy tandem, the breeze nudging them up the hills. Traffic on the river bridge didn't seem as loud as the day before, and Marty barely noticed the smell from the factory or the odor that hung around the dump.

When they arrived at the shelter, Marty stopped his bike in front of the sign with the umbrella picture painted on it. It was a nice picture, really. Sort of cozy looking with all those animals jammed in under an umbrella.

"We should get T-shirts and draw this picture on them," he said, pointing. "We could wear them when we're out finding homes for the animals."

"I'd want pink," said Leanne. "It's full of warm energy, you know."

No, he didn't know.

"Yellow, on the other hand, is irritating. I stay away from yellow. You should too, Marty."

He stood on one pedal and then balanced as his bike glided down the driveway and into the parking lot. Behind him Leanne was rattling on.

As he slipped his bike into the rack, Marty saw

the man with the curly hair, the one they'd met the day before. He got out of an old station wagon.

"You're back," he said.

"We're going to be volunteers," announced Leanne. She waved the application in the air.

Marty counted the cracks in the sidewalk.

When they reached the front door, the man pulled it open. "Be with you in a minute," he said as they walked in. Then he disappeared into the office.

While they stood at the counter, Marty looked around the lobby. There were things he hadn't noticed the day before. A display of dog toys, chew sticks, and catnip mice. A large blue poster that said BE RESPONSIBLE! SPAY/NEUTER YOUR PETS! And to his delight, he saw a row of golden trophies. They stood on a shelf above the office door. He was too far away to read the lettering, but that didn't matter. He could guess who they were for. Volunteers like him. Winners with the animals.

My, how things worked out when you followed your heart.

The man walked out of the office then, and Leanne handed him the application.

Marty pressed one finger against the speckled Formica counter.

"I see you're from Pittsburgh," the man said. "Nice place?"

"We liked Kansas lots better," answered Leanne quickly. "Kansas City, that is. We lived in two different suburbs. Right, Marty?"

A tingle of nerves rolled through Marty's stomach. "Right."

"Well, I'm glad you're here now. I'm Chris, the manager. I'll take you on a tour."

The phone rang then, and Chris turned back to the office. He dropped the application on a stack of papers and turned away from it.

Marty leaned back against the counter, relieved. He listened to the barking from behind the hall door and wished he could go right to the kennel room. Champ would be anxious to see him. But he had to wait a minute. And since he was curious, he said to Leanne, "Did you really live in all those places?"

She looked surprised. "Sure I did. You think I go around making stuff up? I've lived in Florida, too."

"Gee," said Marty. He'd always lived in the house on Fox Lane. "Why?"

"My dad gets new jobs. It's not easy to make money these days, you know."

Marty was grateful, suddenly, for his dad's furniture store. "You must go to a lot of schools."

"Tons. Aunt Jen wants me to live with her. She thinks I should stay in one place. But I don't know. My dad gets lonesome."

Marty blinked. Not live with your parents? He couldn't imagine it. "What about your mom?"

Leanne smoothed her hair away from her face. "It's just me and my dad."

Chris returned then. "Marty? Leanne?" He walked out from behind the counter. "Let's go."

They put green volunteer vests on over their shirts. Then they followed Chris through the shelter as he showed them what to do and where things were. Although he kept saying "don't do this" and "don't do that," Marty saw him smile at every animal they passed, and it made him wish again that he hadn't had to lie on the application.

"One thing we always tell new volunteers," said Chris as he led the way down the hall. "All decisions regarding animal placement are confidential. It's shelter policy. There are no exceptions." He stopped and looked at them. "Will that be a problem?"

"Heck, no," said Marty as he watched a staff person cross the hall with an armload of puppies.

Leanne shook her head.

It was one of the rules, Chris explained, that kept things running smoothly. There were others, too, that kept everyone healthy and safe. He recited them as they walked from one room to the next. Marty memorized each one. (If school was as interesting as this, nobody would ever call him a dawdler!)

When Chris led them into the second kennel room, Marty stopped in front of Champ's stall. "Yo, Champ!" he said.

Champ leaped and hit the water bucket.

Marty reached through the wire fencing of the stall door and patted Champ's nose. An "Adopt ME!" card, he saw, had been clipped to the door. It said *Unclaimed stray.* At the bottom was written the date, the following week, when Champ would be adoptable.

Marty looked into Champ's clear brown eyes. He was glad Champ couldn't read.

"I'll be back, Champ," he whispered. Then he hurried to catch up to Chris.

In the cat room Marty turned a full circle trying to count the number of cages, three tiers high, that lined the walls. Music like he'd heard at Orchestra Hall played out from a radio on a shelf.

"It calms them," said Chris before Marty had the chance to ask.

They met another volunteer, a Girl Scout named Elizabeth. She was working toward her eighth badge, she said as she dusted flea powder over the neck and body of a tiny calico. Marty had to pull Leanne away.

"But, Marty," she said. "She looked like my Jupiter. Even the tail."

In other rooms Chris opened cupboards (dog dishes, towels, shampoo) and drawers (tweezers, cat toys, rubber gloves). On shelves there were bottles of cleaning solutions, stacks of rags, leashes, collars, garbage-can liners, and rawhide chew bones, and in the supply room more of everything.

At the end of the hall, past the kennel rooms and the cat room and the puppy cages, was a door that said STAFF ONLY.

Marty touched the knob as they walked by. It was locked.

"There's so much to remember," Chris was saying as he showed them the coiled hoses used for spraying the kennel floors. "If you forget how to do something, don't worry. Just ask."

"That's a relief," said Leanne.

Marty hummed under his breath, notes from the music he'd heard at Orchestra Hall. Da-da-da-*da*. He wasn't going to need any help at all. He hadn't forgotten a thing. This was the most wonderful place he'd ever seen . . . except for the messages on the "Adopt ME!" cards. It was even better than the zoo. Because here he could touch everybody.

And there was a lot of everybody.

Not only dogs and cats and puppies and kittens but rabbits and hamsters and guinea pigs and mice. Sometimes, Chris said, they even got snakes.

"Cool," said Marty.

"Ugh," said Leanne.

They finished their tour in the laundry room, where the list of daily duties was posted. Marty scanned it: *Clean cages. Feed cats. Sweep floors. Walk dogs. Give baths. Spray kennels.* And on it went.

"As you can see," said Chris, "there's a lot to do."

Marty tapped first one foot then the other. He could hardly wait.

"After you've finished a task," continued Chris, "check it off the list. When your shift is over, drop your vest into the machine. We launder everything."

"Everything?" asked Leanne.

"Everything," said Chris. "Even chew toys and tennis balls. And always wash your hands after you've handled an animal."

Marty smiled to himself. His mother would love this place. Someday he'd show it to her.

"Any more questions?" asked Chris.

Leanne said no.

"Me neither," said Marty.

"Well then," said Chris. He reached out and shook first Leanne's hand and then Marty's. "Welcome to the family, you two."

"It's an honor," said Leanne.

"Yeah. An honor," echoed Marty.

And it was.

He gazed around the room at the stack of dog bowls and litter pans drying from the dishwasher, and the aquarium soaking in the sink. There was a bag of Rabbit Chow propped in the corner, and hamster wheels set in a row on the counter like rides for a miniature amusement park.

He leaned against the side of the rumbling washer and let his breath out long and slow.

He'd never imagined a family as wonderful as this. What did it matter if he'd had to lie to get in?

"Where would you like to start?" asked Chris.

"The cat room," said Leanne. "With Elizabeth."

"Remember where the gloves are?"

Leanne hesitated.

Marty pointed to the third drawer.

Leanne pulled it open and took out a pair of orange rubber gloves. "See ya," she said, and she disappeared around the corner.

"How about you, Marty?" asked Chris.

Marty stared up at the duty list. "Kennel room B, if that's okay. I want to see the Bernard cross."

Chris nodded. "Go for it."

Marty did. He jogged down the hall toward the kennel room like a runner doing a victory lap. "Da-da-da-*da*," he sang as he passed the door to the lobby. "Da-da-da-*daaa*."

When he rounded the corner and turned into the kennel room, he knew for certain that if the day got much greater, he'd pop.

# 10

# Twenty-five Hours a Day

The instant Marty stepped into kennel room B, the ruckus began. Yelps, woofing, high-pitched barks, and a howl echoed off the cement-block walls and reverberated around the room until, for a minute, Marty had to cover his ears. It was wonderful. They were noisier than Twins fans at the Metrodome.

He went to Champ's stall first.

Ignoring the "Adopt ME!" card that hung on the door (who needed to read that again?), he unlatched the hook and stepped in.

Champ nearly knocked him over. He stood like a tower on his hind legs, his front paws on Marty's shoulders.

"Hey, giant puppy. How they treatin' ya?"

Champ licked his ear.

"Good."

Marty gave him a full-minute bear hug. With closed eyes he breathed in the warmth of dog and the faint scent of Glorious Nights. He rubbed his face against the wisps of fur that tickled his cheek.

If only his dad and Francine had felt this! No way would they have let Champ go. He should have made them pet him. Maybe he still could. If only he could think of a way.

He eased the huge front paws off his shoulders and stepped out of the stall. "I'll be back."

Champ stuck his large black nose through the fencing of his door and whined.

"I mean it, really. I'll be right back."

Slowly Marty walked the length of the room. Tails wooshed. Eyes sparkled. The oversized kennel on the end held a mother dog. Her puppies toppled over each other to reach him.

"One big happy family," he said, bending to touch their airy fur. "That's us."

Well, not quite.

The red dog in the kennel next to Champ's was curled in a ball, her head tucked snugly into the curve of her leg. She hadn't wooshed or sparkled or even stood to greet him.

He knelt in front of her door. "Hey, pretty girl," he said. "Don't you wanna come see me?"

She blinked warily.

Marty frowned. Obviously she was still spooked from the ride in the Animal Control truck. "I'll sit with you later," he promised. "You'll feel better then."

She looked away, and Marty walked back to Champ. As he unlatched the hook, Champ rose on his hind legs, as if he wanted another hug, but Marty said, "Not now, Champ. It's time to work."

The stall was narrow. And with Champ in it, Marty could barely turn around. He pulled on the cord attached to the small trapdoor that led to the kennel's outside run, but Champ didn't want to go outside. Or maybe, thought Marty as he looked more closely at the size of the door, he wouldn't fit.

A boy volunteer walked into the kennel room then, and Marty motioned, above the ruckus that had started up again, for help. "Could you take this guy out so I can clean?" he tried to holler louder than the barking.

"Sure," the boy hollered back. He pointed at Champ. "He's cool, isn't he?"

"The coolest."

"Guess how much he weighs."

Marty ran one hand the length of Champ's massive body, then yelled, "Eighty maybe?"

The boy shook his head. "A hundred and nine. Chris says he'll top out over one forty. I'll go get a leash."

Marty smoothed the fur on one of Champ's ears. "Geez, Champ," he said. "You're gonna be bigger than my dad."

Once he was alone in the stall, Marty could maneuver easily. Using a scoop with a long handle, he cleaned the back of Champ's kennel floor. He sprayed it with disinfectant. Then he dragged over one of the coiled hoses, and standing on the lip of the cement, he pressed the nozzle button. Hot water funneled up the hose and shot out across the floor in a sharp jet stream. Marty hung on tight as he watched the water foam and swirl into the middle of the stall, and then disappear down the center drain. He was amazed. The cement was spotless in less than a minute.

He refilled the empty water bucket and set it, this time, in the back corner of the stall so Champ wouldn't knock it over every five seconds. Then he went to find Champ.

On his way out he peeked in the cat room. The Girl Scout volunteer was arranging newspapers on the bottom of a cage. Leanne, in a chair, was covered with kittens. One perched on her shoulder, another draped around her neck, three were asleep in her lap.

"Hi," he called over the orchestra music.

"Shhh!" The girls glared.

Quietly he backed out of the room and closed the door.

Champ was in one of the fenced yards. When he saw Marty, he bounded to the gate and danced there until Marty let himself in.

Champ was not, it turned out, part retriever. Each time Marty tossed him a tennis ball, Champ chased it like you'd expect a dog to do, but then instead of picking it up and bringing it back, he sat on it. As if he were hatching an egg.

After four tries Marty gave up. He plopped down on the step and let his chin rest in his hands. Immediately Champ lumbered over—minus the tennis ball—and they sat, eye to eye.

"Guess you don't know fetch," said Marty.

Champ tipped his head, listening.

"Not that it's a big deal. I mean, I'd keep you any-way, even if you didn't know a thing. Lots of people have dogs who don't know anything."

Marty slipped his fingers through the wavy fur of Champ's neck and Champ yawned.

"But my family's not like that, see. In my family, you gotta know stuff. In my family, you gotta be good at things. A guy can't just sit around."

Champ yawned wider.

Gently Marty patted one floppy ear. "If you were a winner, Champ, my family would adopt you in a second."

He tried to picture Champ in a competition, win-ning a prize for something. But when he looked at Champ's sagging eyelids, the picture fizzled.

Champ was falling asleep sitting up.

Marty roused him, then led him back to his ken-nel via the laundry room. In the cupboard marked LARGE DOG BLANKETS he found a tattered rug. He ar-ranged it neatly in Champ's stall. "Now you can take a nap," he said to Champ as he closed the latch to the stall. "Dream about me."

Out in the hallway there was a contest going on. A battle of wills. It was the boy volunteer versus the hunting dog who wouldn't hunt. They were pulling on either end of a leash that looked ready to snap.

"She's supposed to have a bath," grunted the boy, who was leaning backward to make use of his weight. "But I don't know." His fingers, twisted around his end of the leash, were turning white.

The dog, on the other end, was hunkered in a forget-it-I-hate-water crouch. Her eyes bulged from the strain.

"I'll help," said Marty, and he ran to the supply room for the box of Yum-yum dog treats. *Positively Irresistible* it said across the lid. Marty dug for the biggest, then raced back. "What's her name?"

"Pepper."

"Hi ya, Pepper. How 'bout this?" Marty dangled the bone-shaped treat in the air.

She cocked one eye toward him, but she didn't move a muscle.

Marty opened his mouth, and pretended to take a bite. "That is *goooood.*"

"Yeah, Pepper," said the boy, huffing. "Pup treat!"

She looked back and forth from Marty to the boy to the treat.

Marty took a step closer. "Here, Pepper," he coaxed. "Take a bite."

She raised up for only a second, and the boy pulled her forward. Her nails clicked as they slid along the tile. It went on like that, a few inches at a time, until they hoisted her into the empty tub and gave her the treat.

"I haven't seen you here before," said the boy as he ran the hand sprayer along Pepper's back.

"It's my first day," said Marty.

The boy's name was Arthur Finley. He lived on the west side of town.

"Hi," said Marty, holding tight the wriggling Pepper. And then, because he wasn't sure if he should say Hobarth or Igler, he answered only, "I'm Marty." He worked the shampoo into a froth on Pepper's back.

They took turns with the hand sprayer, washing and then rinsing her down. By the time they were finished, the fronts of their green volunteer vests were soaked. Pepper's coat was smooth and glossy.

When Arthur invited him over sometime, Marty said, "I don't get to the west side much." The truth was, he never got to the west side. His mother didn't let him bike that far.

But Arthur said he had a ferret. Its name was Bandit and it slept in a hat.

Marty had never seen a ferret. And his mother was in Mexico. "Maybe I will," he said to Arthur, on his way back to the kennel room. "Thanks."

He was in the midst of things when Leanne tapped him on the shoulder.

"Marty," she said. "It's lunchtime. Did you bring something? I'm hungry."

Marty set the mop in the bucket and looked up at the wall clock. Where had the morning gone?

As if on cue Leanne's stomach rumbled. "See? I'm not kidding. We were gonna look for homes in the afternoon anyway. That was the plan, wasn't it?"

"Yeah," he said, remembering. That was the plan.

It had been his idea. Volunteer at the shelter in the morning, find homes for the animals in the afternoon. Only he couldn't possibly leave yet. He hadn't been to the other kennel room. He needed to spend time with the mother dogs and their puppies. Plus there was the red dog to think of. And Champ. He certainly wasn't ready to leave Champ.

Besides. What was the rush? They had plenty of time to look for homes.

He brushed dog hair off the front of his vest, which was still damp from Pepper's bath, and said, "Let's not start that part today. I've still got stuff to do."

"Well, I'm leaving. I want to ask Aunt Jen's apartment manager why he doesn't let anybody have pets. I don't think that's fair, do you?"

"No." But it sure was familiar.

"Can you find your way home?"

What did she think he was? Some dumb baby?

Deftly Marty pushed down and then up on the handle of the squeegee. Water gushed from the mop. "This is Marty Igler you're talking to, remember? I've lived in Pittsburgh and Kansas and all over the place. You think I can't handle this shrimpy town?"

She rolled her eyes. "Okay, brother," she said. "See ya tomorrow."

He stayed the rest of the day. He cleaned more dog kennels, which, at midday, was a hot and stinky job. He sang to the red dog. With Arthur, he fed guinea pigs, changed hamster bedding, and swept floors. Then he sat with the mother dog in kennel room B and let her puppies climb on his legs and perform daring leaps off his ankles.

His green vest dried. He forgot to eat. At the end of the afternoon, he took Champ on a walk around the block.

At four o'clock, his stomach hollow and grumbling, he took off his vest and dropped it in the washing machine. Then he pushed open the glass front door of the shelter and shuffled out to his bike.

Just the thought of the long ride home made him feel sleepy. If he cut straight through town, just this once, he could be home in half the time.

He decided to do it.

As he pedaled past the dump and across the iron walkway of the bridge, it was easy to let his mind drift. He thought of the twitching noses of the guinea pigs. The tumbling puppies. The twinkle in Champ's eyes.

He watched the grooves of his front tire spin as he thought about the red dog. Maybe what she needed was something to keep her company. He could bring her something from home. Like his old teddy bear or his turtle pillow. He certainly didn't need those things anymore. He was deciding between them when he heard the honking of a horn.

He shook the haze from his mind and looked up.

He was in the middle of an intersection. Coming toward him, in the right lane, was a white van. A van just like his dad's.

He jammed on his brakes. A surge of dread rolled through his stomach. With a gulp he forced himself to look up at the driver.

It was a woman in a flowered shirt.

It was not his dad.

But it could have been!

*"Fool kid!"* hollered someone. *"Get outta the road!"* hollered someone else. More horns began to blare.

Furiously he pumped across the blacktop, the muscles in his legs knotting like fists. The wind plastered his hair against his forehead. *Pong! Pong!* His tires sped over the metal plate of a manhole cover. He jumped the curb, nearly flying, and swerved into the entryway of a bank. He screeched to a halt, gasping.

In the reflection of the display window, he saw the stoplight change and the traffic speed past him. Instinctively he pressed himself up flat against the side of the brick doorway, one foot still on the pedal of his bike, his pulse pounding in his ears.

What was he doing out there in the middle of town plain as day for everyone to see? What if that *had* been his dad? I mean, it almost was!

Even worse, he'd pedaled into a swarm of traffic without even looking. He could have been run over.

He let his head bump back against the bricks and

wiped the perspiration off his forehead as he tried not to imagine getting run over. Or the front page of the *Gazette.*

> Lawrence Martin Hobarth, formerly known as Marty the Zilch, wrecked everything and disappointed everybody for the last time today. He is now a pancake on Madison and Fifth. Bring the scraper.

Heat rose in his cheeks. He closed his eyes and tried not to think about being a pancake. He tried even harder not to think about his dad.

He stayed pressed against the side of the building, the back of his shirt damp against his shoulder blades, for a long time. He'd learned one thing for certain. Bad things could still happen if he didn't watch out.

But they weren't going to.

He'd be on alert twenty-five hours a day, if that's what it took, because following your heart, he knew now, meant you couldn't relax for a second.

# 11

# The Rescuer

In the week that followed, Marty decided that almost getting mashed into a pancake hadn't been all bad. It had been a warning that made him cautious. A warning that made him wise. Best of all, it helped him remember to *think* before he did things.

Which was nothing to sneeze at.

Because after years of being told to do so by his mother and his dad, he finally, on his own, turned his life into an organized, busy routine.

He put himself on a schedule.

It began before breakfast when he slipped on his swimsuit and draped his beach towel around his neck, as if he were going to spend the day at the pool. It ended in the late afternoon when, on his way home, he rode through the boulevard sprinklers for a good soaking. In case his dad or Francine had any doubts.

He'd thought of everything in between, too.

Each day he and Leanne biked to the shelter the long way. They went back to wearing sunglasses. And Marty started carrying his school backpack, in which he stuffed his lunch, and snacks, and anything else from home that he thought the animals might need. Like his turtle pillow, which he'd dug out of his old toy chest and given to the red dog. Like the toys he bought for Champ.

In the mornings they did their volunteer work. In the afternoons they split up. Leanne rang doorbells of the residents in the apartment building. When the apartment manager had told her people didn't really need pets, she'd stomped back to Aunt Jen's apartment and made a petition. Then she'd started collecting signatures.

And Marty kept busy at the shelter. Cleaning, feeding, walking, scooping.

"Why aren't you out looking for dog homes yet?" Leanne had asked him one morning on their way to the river bridge.

He'd shrugged off her question. Everything was so nice at the shelter. All the animals were fine. Besides, he'd written a note on Champ's "Adopt ME!" card that said, *This dog is reserved. Marty Igler will adopt soon.*

"But Champ's going to need a home, Marty. You can't hog him forever."

"I know that. But my dad's gonna change his mind real soon now." He'd tried to sound confident.

"What if he doesn't?"

Marty hadn't answered. He was waiting for the next thing to turn up that would make it happen. The next magic thing. The fortune cookie wasn't going to let him down now, was it?

No.

The next something came on Friday when Leanne presented him with a book called *Remarkable Dogs.*

"I went to the library," she said when Marty emerged, dripping, from under the boulevard sprinkler. "And I found this." She waved a book in front of his eyes. "It's loaded with information, especially page forty-seven." She fanned the pages in front of him. "See what I mean?"

"Not exactly," said Marty.

"There's even a famous dog who vaults fire."

Marty dried his face with his beach towel and tried to imagine Champ vaulting fire.

"Well, here." She handed him the book. "You can read it over the weekend. Especially page forty-seven."

He shoved the book into his pack. Then they turned their bikes toward home.

That evening, after he'd read the postcard that had arrived from Mom (*Dear darlings. Not much progress here. I miss you. Hope all is well!*), he dried the dinner dishes and mowed the front yard. When he came back in the house, he said, "Good night, everybody," and climbed the stairs to his room. He closed the door and sat on the floor by the terrarium. With a large bag of M & Ms in his lap, one of the tree frogs on his shoulder, and Godzilla dozing on his knee, he opened the book.

Leanne had been right. It was loaded.

As he turned the pages, he saw pictures of dogs

that herded sheep and dogs that sniffed out bur-
glars. Dogs that guarded castles and dogs that
helped people who couldn't see. There was a whole
section on dogs that made commercials for television.

Marty picked up the bag of M & Ms and tore it
open with his teeth. Champ would be good on television. His family would love that.

But how would he get Champ to Hollywood?

He lifted the bag and tipped it into his mouth.
M & Ms rolled onto his tongue. He crunched down
on them as he read the story about the dog who
vaulted a blazing pole. His name was Roger the
Magnificent. He lived in the circus.

Marty stared at the picture of Roger, mid-leap.
The flames looked dangerous. He, Marty, would
never let Champ do that. Even if it would make him
famous.

He popped more M & Ms into his mouth and
chewed them. Then he remembered Leanne's ad-
vice and turned to page forty-seven.

He almost choked on the candy.

It was a picture of a full-blooded Saint Bernard.
Massive, speckled, beautiful, the dog had a splotch
of brown fur on his side the shape of Texas.

The picture took up the whole page. It looked a
lot like Champ.

Not exactly, but a lot.

Page forty-eight was the text. It was titled "The
Rescuer."

Reverently Marty whispered the words. Then he read the paragraph below.

> *Saint Bernards are the champions of rescue operations. Intelligent and gentle, they are trained to find people trapped in snowdrifts and avalanches. They stay close to the victims to keep them warm, licking their faces to stimulate circulation. Many people owe their lives to one of these remarkable heroes.*

Marty let his breath escape with a "Yes!" as he stared down at the page. This was it, without question. The something he was supposed to do next. Train Champ to be a hero.

He closed his eyes and imagined his dad and his mother and Francine stuck in a snowdrift. A huge one like they'd had in the yard after last winter's blizzard. He imagined everyone in town looking for them but Champ finding them. And digging them out. And then faithfully licking their faces. "Thank heavens we had Champ," his father would say when they were all safe inside the house. "He saved our lives."

The scene rolled before Marty's eyes like the preview of an upcoming movie. The grateful sound in his father's voice made him tingly with pride. He rubbed at the goosebumps on his arms.

Pretty soon his dad was going to *beg* to adopt Champ. Because heroes, everybody knew, were even better than winners.

Marty leaned back against the bookshelf and whispered, "Yeah, Mom. Everything's going great."

Of course he'd never trained a dog before. But it shouldn't be too hard. In fact, it should be fun. There was probably a book that told you how to do it. All he had to do was go to the library and find it.

"Marty?"

It was his dad, outside the bedroom door. The surprise of it jolted him, and M & Ms from the bag in his lap spilled across the floor. On his knee, Godzilla bobbed his head in alarm.

"Are you still awake, son?"

Marty's pulse pounded like a drum. A voice inside his head whispered, "Tell him! Right now! Show him the book!"

He looked down at Godzilla, whose bright pink throat fan was thrust out, ready for attack. Godzilla, who was not supposed to be out of the terrarium.

"Marty?"

"Yeah, Dad. I'm awake." He shoved some of the M & Ms under his leg. He'd have to pretend the lizard wasn't there and hope his dad wouldn't notice. He spread his hands over page forty-seven as his father opened the door.

"Ah," he said. "You're reading."

Framed in the doorway, his dad looked even taller than usual. Marty could feel perspiration dampen the palms of his hands. He pressed them against the page as he tried to smile. Inside his head the voice had changed. Now it was telling him not to say a word. That he wasn't ready. That he'd screw it up.

"I won't interrupt, Marty. I just came to say that I need you and Francine at the F & A tomorrow, with your mother gone. It needs a good cleaning. We'll play miniature golf later and go for pizza. Would you like to invite someone from the team along?"

"The team?"

"How about David Bock?"

Marty hadn't thought about David or the diving team in days. He glanced down at his sweating hands. "Everybody's pretty busy, Dad."

"It'll just be the three of us then. Oh, and I'm going to Chicago for a few days next week. A furniture show. Mrs. Prinzig will be staying here." His dad took a step closer and peered down. "What's that on your shoulder? It's moving."

The tree frog! He'd forgotten all about it. And he couldn't pick it off because his hands were covering page forty-seven. "Just a little guy, Dad."

"For heaven's sake, Marty. Where do frogs belong?"

"Outside."

"And him?" His dad pointed at Godzilla.

"In the terrarium."

"Take care of it right now, Marty." His dad turned and took hold of the doorknob. "And you know better than to eat up here."

Marty nodded. After his dad left, he scooped up

Godzilla and the tree frog and set them on the electric rock. "Hide," he said to the frog. Then he replaced the lid of the terrarium and stood up.

It had gotten hot in his room.

He yanked off his pajama top, wiped his hands on it, and let it drop to the floor. Then he stepped around a few stray M & Ms to his windowsill. He turned the crank hard until the window was open full. He shivered as the breeze sailed across his chest.

Why did it always happen like that? He'd be doing just fine until his dad showed up. Then he turned into Jell-O. Stupid, shivering Jell-O.

He took the remarkable dog book to bed with him and slid it under his pillow. It was flat and hard against his head, but he didn't care. It would help him think about Champ instead of his dad.

Right now he, Marty, was the one who needed the rescuer.

He squeezed his eyes shut and hoped for dog dreams.

# 12

# The F & A

**M**arty watched out the passenger window of the van as his dad drove them down the main street of Johnson Falls. The storefronts and businesses looked asleep in the early morning, with their shades drawn and their blinds closed.

Next to him in the front seat, Francine was chattering away about something, but he wasn't listening. Even though he was glad she was there, sitting in the middle, between his father and himself.

It gave him room to think. About the shelter, where he couldn't go, and Champ, whom he couldn't see, because it was Saturday. Family day.

He needed to buck up. It was not a day to be Jell-O.

"Skooch over, Marty," said Francine.

"I can't," he answered. "I'm on the edge already."

He watched the striped awnings of Fandel's department store ripple in the breeze as they drove past. Then he caught a glimpse of himself in the van's side mirror, his hair blown back against his forehead.

He looked like a kid who did not want to be where he was.

He forced a smile.

Now he looked like a kid who did not want to be where he was but was faking it.

Next to him Francine was laughing. His dad, too. They never worried about anything.

He propped his elbow on the window ledge and let his chin rest in his hand. He wished he was on his way to the shelter. He hoped Leanne would remember to play with Champ and to sit with the red dog, like she'd promised. He wished he could talk to her about page forty-seven, too.

"Marty?"

Marty turned to his dad.

"I was telling Francine. When I get home from Chicago, we'll go to the lake for a few days. Have some fun."

Marty tapped his fingers against his cheek. How would he get Champ trained to be a hero if he had to go to the lake and have fun?

"Another thing." His dad was still talking. "When I get home I'm going to visit you at the pool."

Marty lurched forward. *"What?"*

"I want to see my Olympic diver in action."

"You do?"

"Of course."

Marty's stomach, pressed against the seat belt, felt like it had just been punched. "But, Dad. The coach said."

"I'm sure he won't mind now. Besides, I'll just watch."

Marty dug his fingernails into the foam armrest

as he pictured his dad at the pool, talking to the coach, hearing the horrible truth. "The kid bombed, Mr. Hobarth. Totally. I haven't seen him since the tryouts."

Marty blinked. Outside the window, the stores along the street were a blur.

"I'll bet you're getting good, too." Mr. Hobarth reached behind Francine and patted Marty's shoulder.

Marty sagged back against the seat and held his stomach.

"Told ya not to eat M & Ms for breakfast," said Francine.

"You ate candy for breakfast, Marty?"

"Yup," answered Francine. "He did. It was d-i-s-g-u-s-t-i-n-g. Disgusting."

"I should have stayed home and scrambled some eggs." Mr. Hobarth had done his usual seven miles. "Muscles need protein."

"So do brains," added Francine.

Marty didn't feel like he had either muscles or brains. He rubbed at the waistband of his jeans and burped chocolate. If he looked in the side mirror, he knew his face would be green. "When exactly do you get home from the trip?" he managed to ask.

"Wednesday."

That was five days. Five measly days.

They passed Foo Chu Express. Marty wished he could run in and get another fortune cookie. One that could tell you how to do a miracle. Because nobody could turn a dog into a hero in five days, no matter how many books he read. Nobody.

The van slowed. Mr. Hobarth switched on his signal and turned into the alley behind the store. At once they were in shadow, rumbling past sooty back walls of buildings and dumpsters and swirling bits of paper.

Marty clutched at his stomach. What could he possibly do in five days to make everything turn out right? What?

The van came to a stop behind the store.

"Okay, troops," said Mr. Hobarth to both Marty and Francine. "Let's get at it."

Marty released his seat belt and took a last look in the side mirror. "Come on, Hobarth," he mouthed silently to the pale face staring back at him. "You gotta think." Then he pulled on the handle and climbed down from the van.

He stood in the alley while he waited for his dad to unlock the door and pictured Champ pacing in his stall at the shelter. Champ, who was counting on him. Champ, who needed him to think!

When Mr. Hobarth opened the door, Marty followed him in.

The back room was cluttered with lamps and boxes and new pieces of furniture shrink-wrapped in plastic. Marty walked around a grocery cart stacked with framed pictures.

Francine lifted her radio headphones, which had been dangling from around her neck, and settled them over her ears. She reached for the feather duster.

Mr. Hobarth went into the office. "Catch the lights for me, Mart."

Marty walked through the darkened showroom, around bedroom groupings and kitchen sets and his mother's favorite dining-room table, named after some queen, to the electrical panel on the side wall. He flipped the lever for the lights. Then he pressed the switches for the ceiling fans and watched as they began to spin above him like a row of airplane propellers.

Usually when he came down to the F & A, he liked to sit in the recliner chairs or test the mattresses or read comics in an empty furniture carton. But not today. Today he couldn't just sit around. Today he had to think up a miracle.

He headed for the vacuum cleaner.

He plugged in the extension cord and gripped the rubber handle. When he kicked the power pedal with his foot, the old machine roared. He pushed it hard across the sample indoor/outdoor carpet, its headlight winking, the attachment bag swollen like an oblong balloon. Then he yanked it back toward him, not slowing for glitches in the rug or packing strings or even tacks.

When he passed Francine, dusting the face of a grandfather clock, she lifted one headphone away from her ear and motioned for him to shut off the motor.

"Marty," she said, her voice suspicious. "What's the deal with you?"

"Huh?"

"You're working."

Marty shrugged.

"You're up to something, aren't you?"

He almost wished he could tell her. She was smart at finding answers, although he'd never tell her he thought so. But he couldn't. Because she'd tell Dad and then it would be two against one, as usual.

"Move, will ya?" he said. He pushed the power pedal on-off-on, and the motor revved. "I'm busy."

He was a maniac, maneuvering the heavy machine around couches and down aisles, dipping under tables and lifting wicker chairs with one hand. If he'd been in a vacuum-cleaner race, he would have won. But he still didn't know what he was going to do.

Maybe he'd just have to confess. Tell his dad everything. Like he probably should have done on the porch that night.

"Marty." His dad's voice boomed over the store's intercom. "Come here, will you?"

Marty took a deep breath. It was not the time to be Jell-O. He unplugged the vacuum and dragged it behind him, past the row of recliner chairs, to the back room.

His dad had removed the plastic wrap from a small two-seat sofa.

"Help me get this out front, Marty," he said. "Remember to lift with your legs."

Marty curled his fingers under the wood frame. "Okay, Dad. I'm ready."

They shuffled down the center aisle of the store. Marty took short breaths and small steps and kept his gaze steady—just like his dad had taught him. He didn't wobble once. They placed the sofa near the front window, next to a painted rocker. When Marty let go finally and stood up, his dad was smiling at him.

"Good job, son," he said.

"Thanks." Marty smoothed his hand over the striped cushion of the sofa and smiled back. Maybe he ought to tell his dad right then while he was acting happy. They could sit down together on the sofa. He could start with how Saint Bernards saved lives—when you had time to train them.

But thought of it made his mouth go dry.

The phone rang in the office.

"Collect the carpet samples, Marty. Here's the first one." His dad handed him a small square of rosy carpet and turned toward the office.

Marty slumped down onto the sofa. He smoothed his hand over the soft knots of the rug sample. "Strawberry Fizz, by Majestic," he read on the back. He hugged it to his chest.

Collecting the carpet samples from all over the store, where customers had left them, was a job his mother usually did. Marty missed her. He wished she were there. She never made him feel like Jell-O.

Maybe he'd write her a letter when they got home. Tell *her* about how Saint Bernards could save your life. He could draw her a picture and give her a few facts. Mention the snowdrift. Then, when she was out digging dirt, she could be thinking dog. By the time she got home, she'd be ready for one.

Hey.

Why not get them *all* thinking dog? Ease them into it. Without giving it away, of course. Nothing big. Just a few hints. Then, when they were ready, he'd tell them about Champ. Maybe that's what had gone wrong the day he'd brought Champ home. He'd been too big a surprise!

Marty put his feet up on on a coffee table and let the idea wash over him. Not only was it good, but it would let him get started on the truth. Which would certainly be a relief.

And so, after he finished with the carpet samples, he began to rearrange things in the F & A. Small things.

He took down paintings of flowers and replaced them with framed dog pictures he found in the grocery cart in the back. (There were lots! Somebody around here really did like dogs!)

He found dog bookends, which he set on the table next to the new sofa, and a large doorstop, a brass collie, which he dragged up the center aisle and set next to the front door. There were glass poodles and some small carved things that looked sort of like dogs, which he placed on different ledges and tables here and there. Then he walked to the accessories corner.

He'd saved the best for last.

In front of the candlesticks was a statue he'd noticed a long time ago. Way before he'd met Champ or Leanne or even before his mother had gone to Mexico. It was a great fringed dog with a pheasant in his mouth.

Gently Marty lifted it off the shelf. Carefully he carried it across the room. Holding his breath, he set it in the center of the dining table of the queen. Then he stood back and scanned the showroom.

There were dogs everywhere.

His dad and Francine couldn't help but see them. Or touch them. Or even bump into one, like the doorstop.

He flexed the muscles in his arms. With any luck, tonight they would have dog dreams too.

# 13

# Garbage

**M**arty stood with Francine and Mrs. Prinzig on the front porch and waved as his dad drove down Fox Lane, on his way to Chicago.

After the car went around the curve and was out of sight, Marty crossed his fingers behind his back and made a wish for good luck. Because in the glove box of the car, on top of his dad's maps, Marty'd stashed a note. A special note, which included a drawing of a Saint Bernard and a list of lifesaving facts that every owner should know. Marty hoped it would give him powerful dog thoughts.

"Francine," said Mrs. Prinzig. "I suppose you're off to your class."

"Yes! And I'm late!" Francine scooped her books off the porch swing and hurried down the sidewalk.

Mrs. Prinzig turned to Marty. "And you're on your way to the pool, I see."

"Yup." Marty patted his beach towel, which hung around his neck. He was sorry to have to lie to Mrs. Prinzig. But it was a lot easier than doing it to his dad.

"I packed you a lunch, Marty. It's on the kitchen

table." Mrs. Prinzig put her hands in the pockets of her apron and smiled. "My Jeffrey used to swim everyday when he was your age. He got awfully hungry. I gave you two sandwiches."

"Thanks, Mrs. P.," he said. He swung open the screen door and headed into the kitchen to pick up his backpack.

He took the letter he'd written to his mother (with her copy of the dog facts and a drawing) out of his pocket and slid it into the pack. His mother would be happy to hear from him. She'd probably read the letter to the other people at the dig. (There wasn't any TV.) They'd tell her how lucky she was to have a son who wrote letters and liked dogs.

He stuffed the sandwiches into the pack, zipped the zipper, and hefted it onto his back. The weight filled him with confidence. Everything was going to work out.

He mailed the letter at the Jiffy Mart. When Leanne arrived, they pushed off toward the shelter. They talked as they pedaled.

"I hope it works," Leanne said when Marty told her about making his family think dog.

He pumped down on one pedal and glided ahead. "It will."

Leanne caught up. "Maybe you should memorize the Saint Bernard section in the dog book. They'll probably start asking questions."

He already had, what with copying it twice.

"Or, Marty." Leanne sat sideways on her bike seat

to face him. "Maybe we could find a book just on Bernards. One with bigger pictures and stories from survivors."

Marty liked the sound of that.

When they reached the hill that led to the river bridge, they climbed off their bikes and began to walk them. "Did you sit with the red dog for me?" Marty asked. "I gave her my turtle pillow."

Leanne slowed. "I forgot to tell you, Marty. She's gone."

"Gone?"

Leanne nodded.

Marty stopped walking. An ache filled his chest. "Who adopted her?"

"I couldn't ask. Remember the rule?"

Of course he remembered. He'd just forgotten for a minute. It was the first rule Chris had told them, the day they'd had their tour through the shelter. All decisions regarding animals were confidential. Volunteers were not to inquire.

Marty adjusted the backpack, which had begun to pull at his shoulders, and then resumed his walking. "I hope they let her keep my pillow," he said. "I told Chris it was for her."

The ache in his chest remained as they crossed the river bridge and pedaled on to the shelter. He knew it was dumb. He knew he ought to be glad she'd found a home. But he couldn't help it. He'd just never pictured going to the shelter and not seeing her.

"Champ's still there, right?" he asked in a flash of panic.

Marty sighed his relief.

"Of course your note wouldn't help much if his owner came in to claim him," reminded Leanne.

Marty pushed ahead of her as they biked past the dump. It was a thought he tried hard not to think.

"Oh, yes. Your note is still on his card."

Over the weekend there'd been several other changes at the shelter, and Marty was sorry again that he'd had to spend the time with his father and Francine. Even if they had played miniature golf and gone out for pizza.

Three of the mother dog's puppies from kennel room A were gone, and Pepper, the hunting dog. A passel of kittens had arrived. And a lone puppy had been left at the side door in a basket. She was so small, she had to be fed with a baby bottle. The staff was crazy over her.

Marty touched the fluffy, rust-colored fur of her head while Nancy, the shift supervisor, held her. Then he went to kennel room B.

"Hi, Champ," he said as he finished buttoning his volunteer vest.

Champ leaped to greet him. Marty gave him a pat through the door. "Just a minute. I gotta see something."

He stepped in front of the red dog's stall. It was empty, all right. A clean water bucket sat upside down in the corner, a signal to the staff that the kennel had been scrubbed and was ready for somebody new. Her "Adopt ME!" card was gone.

Marty poked his fingers through the wire fencing of the stall door. This was one thing, he decided, he didn't like about his new shelter family. At least at home, with his mom and dad and Francine, you knew when someone was leaving and when they'd be home.

He walked back to Champ's stall and stepped in. "Don't be sad," he said as he nuzzled the fur of Champ's neck. "Pretty soon you won't be here either. Pretty soon you'll be at home with me."

He took Champ outside to one of the fenced yards for exercise, to make up for the two days he'd been away. While they played tug with a sock, Marty told him about the dog book. "You're not a stray, Champ. You're a hero. You should be proud." It always helped, his mom said, to know who you were.

The morning rushed by.

It was noon when Marty decided to eat the first of his two sandwiches. He was on his way to the kitchen to get his backpack and a bottle of pop when Arthur grabbed him.

A hamster had escaped.

"I don't know how it happened," said Arthur, agitated. "He was sitting right here just a minute ago." He pointed to a lid that had been removed from one aquarium and was propped up on the shelf. "I went to change his water and he was gone."

"Who is it?"

"Kenny. The fast one."

"Maybe he fell back in," Marty suggested. He bent down and peered in to the aquarium. He looked at the cedar shavings and the nest of fuzz and paper toweling Kenny had built. There was no Kenny.

"We better split up," said Arthur. "I'll check the storage room."

"I'll try the laundry." Marty walked slowly down the hall, looking behind dog crates and brooms for Kenny, or for the telltale pellet droppings he could have left. But there was nothing. When he reached the door to the laundry, he looked in.

No Kenny.

But on the counter, in a pile of clean towels, sat his turtle pillow. Chris had forgotten to send it home with the red dog.

How disappointing.

Marty walked in and picked it up. If he'd worked Saturday, this wouldn't have happened. He rubbed the familiar smooth spot against his chin, until out of the corner of his eye he saw the hamster speed past the doorway.

"Kenny!" Marty tossed the pillow on the counter and hurried after him. He chased the streaking hamster halfway down the hall, and was about to snatch him up when the small furred body flattened itself and slipped under the door of the STAFF ONLY room.

Oh, great.

Marty looked around for Chris, or Nancy, or one of the other staff on duty, but there was no one. He

chewed at a fingernail. If he left to go find somebody, Kenny could get out and be gone and then
maybe they'd never find him.

He tried the knob.

Surprisingly it was unlocked. He turned it all the
way, and the door opened in front of him. Once
again he looked around for someone. The hallway
was empty.

So he went in.

It was an odd room. Different from all the others
at the shelter, quiet except for the whirring of a portable fan. And it smelled funny.

At once Marty wished he was not there. But he
couldn't just leave Kenny. So he took another step
in and closed the door.

In front of him was a double tier of cages, all
empty but two. A mother cat lay in one, surrounded
by fuzzy, balled-up kittens. She stared at him with
marble-green eyes.

The basket puppy was in another cage, a puff of
rusty fur curled on a heating pad, her baby bottle
nearby.

There were dog kennels, too. A dalmatian with a
bandage on his shoulder lay dozing in one.

Marty wished Kenny would just pop out so he
could grab him and be gone. "Kenny!" he whispered, as if hamsters came when you called.

No Kenny, of course. So Marty took a silent step
farther into the room.

Along the back wall was a large white chest
freezer. Next to it was a metal table on wheels.

Above it were shelves crammed full with boxes and bottles.

Could Kenny have climbed up on one?

Careful not to disturb the wounded dalmatian, Marty tiptoed past his kennel toward the shelves. The mother cat, he saw, followed his every step.

On the first shelf were boxes of plastic garbage bags, the heavy-duty kind, and containers of surgical gloves. Rolls of bandage tape and cotton swabs and boxes with pictures of syringes on them. On the second shelf was a row of medicine bottles and sprays.

Things happened in here. Like the dalmatian getting his shoulder fixed. Like shots. And maybe operations. Marty thought about when his appendix was taken out.

"Kenny!" he whispered, more urgently. "I don't have all day!"

He leaned against the cold metal of the table on wheels. Next to it, he saw, was a piece of paper taped to a utility pole. On it was a prayer.

He read it. It was about wisdom. And accepting the things you can't change. He'd heard it before. But why would anybody hang a prayer in a place like this?

He stepped back from the table. If Kenny didn't show up soon, he'd leave without him. He'd go tell Chris. Chris could find him.

He turned a slow circle, looking, listening. And then he heard it. A scratching noise from behind the freezer. He tiptoed over to it and knelt down. He put his head next to the floor and tried to see underneath. He couldn't. But it must have been Kenny. He should have brought some kind of hamster treat.

"Kenny," he whispered. "I know you're under there!"

Just then the freezer's motor cycled on with a clank and the hamster scampered out.

Marty grabbed him. "Who do you think you are, Kenny? Columbus?" he tried to joke.

The hamster's nose twitched. His eyes glistened.

The freezer's motor hummed.

Marty stood up. He could leave now. He could walk across the room and open the door and go back out into the bright hallway.

Except there was the freezer.

At his house there was a freezer in the basement. His mother stored bread in it, and vegetables from her garden, and fish from their trips to the lake.

He wanted to know what was in this one.

He slipped Kenny into the deep front pocket of his vest and petted him quiet. "We'll go in a sec," he whispered, staring down at the freezer.

All he wanted was one peek. Besides, as a volunteer who wanted to do the best job he could, as a winner with the animals, he deserved to know. Right?

Hesitating, he glanced up at the mother cat. Her owl eyes held him. He turned his back to her and lifted the lid.

A heavy odor wafted up. He wrinkled his nose and

looked in. The freezer was full of garbage bags, each one sealed with a bright yellow tie.

How weird.

Breathing through his mouth, he reached down and touched the top bag. The black plastic crinkled. And a shock of recognition shot up his arm like electric current.

It was a leg.

Inside the garbage bag was a leg.

Marty gasped. He yanked his hand back, his pulse hammering. He wanted to run!

But his fingers went back to the bag. Skimming along the plastic, they became his eyes. They followed the curve of the leg, which was folded as if running. Up the body to the shoulder. Back down the leg to the paw.

And in his mind Marty saw the red dog. Her legs tucked, her eyes wide.

He knew it was her.

He stared down at the bag and willed it to move. Willed her to twitch just one paw. *Please, red lady, please.* He begged, his fingers burning from the cold.

But she couldn't move. She was frozen solid.

A shudder rippled through him. Spots twinkled around the edge of his vision. He tried to gulp air, his chest aching for it, but he couldn't.

He had to get out.

He slammed the lid closed and stumbled for the door. He turned the knob, his fingers numb, and pulled. When the door swung open, he burst out into the bright hallway and ran.

Ahead of him, he saw Arthur standing in front of the aquariums. He pulled the hamster out of his pocket and handed him over as he charged by.

"Marty. What's wrong? What happened?"

Marty didn't answer. He couldn't. He had to get out. He raced through the lobby and shoved open the glass front door.

He crossed the parking lot running. He swerved around Chris's station wagon and then more parked cars, skidding on pebbles, gulping mouthfuls of air. He grabbed hold of his bike. With a grunt he swung his leg over the seat and reached for the handlebars. But his volunteer vest had caught on something and held him back. He pulled at it but it wouldn't budge. He turned and saw, bleary-eyed, that the green fabric was hooked to his reflector. He yanked it. He wrenched it. He tore at it until finally, with one seam-rending rip, he was free.

His front tire was still wedged in the slot of the bike rack. He positioned his feet on the blacktop to push himself out. He wrapped his fingers around the ridged rubber of the handle grips. His knuckles, he saw, were bone white. He stared down at them, blinking. Then he lowered his head and began to cry.

There was no stopping it.

He couldn't pedal away because he couldn't see.

And then Leanne was there, and Arthur. Asking, asking, Marty, Marty, what's wrong?

He couldn't tell them. Couldn't mouth the words.

The freezer was full of dead dogs.

# 14

# Walking Billboards

"**M**arty," said Leanne. "Talk to me."

"No." Marty hiccuped, the last remnant of tears.

They were still in the parking lot of the animal shelter. Marty had refused to get off his bike, so Arthur and Leanne stood one on either side of him, coaxing.

"Maybe you made a mistake," said Arthur. "Maybe it wasn't a dog."

"It was a dog."

"But you don't really know it was her," said Leanne.

"I know."

"Why'd you go in there in the first place?" asked Arthur.

"Because you lost the hamster."

"Oh. Yeah."

Marty wished they'd both just go away. He couldn't believe they could work there, knowing what was happening. *Murder!* Right there in the building!

"You guys are both jerks," he said. "Leave me alone."

117

This time it was Leanne who said no. "Why are you mad at us? It's not our fault."

"But you knew."

"I didn't!" sputtered Arthur. "I didn't know one thing!"

"But Marty did." Leanne's eyes flashed. "I told him that first day in the park. Remember, Marty? I said not everybody who goes in comes out."

It was true. But he hadn't let himself think about it. He'd pretended to forget. He glared at Leanne. "Why'd you even want to work here?"

"I didn't want to, Marty. *You* did."

"Well, you shoulda stopped me."

Leanne threw up her arms, exasperated. "You talked me into it. I thought we were just going to save Champ. But you acted like it was some miracle we got to be volunteers."

Marty let his shoulders sag. He thought of Mr. Chu's cookies. And the fortunes. Follow your heart. What a joke.

Leanne pulled a rag out of the pocket of her vest and dabbed her eyes. "I hoped this place would be different. Everybody was so nice."

The front door of the shelter swung open then and some people walked out. Marty straightened up on his bike. Leanne looked away. Arthur bent down to tie his shoelace.

After the people had climbed into their car and driven off, Arthur stood up. "Did you see which dogs were in there, Marty?"

"No."

"It's not just dogs, you know," said Leanne, sniffing.

Arthur slumped against the metal bar of the bike rack. "I hope they're not killing hamsters. You didn't see any small bags in there, did you?"

Marty shook his head.

"They probably put them all together in a big bag," said Leanne.

Arthur moaned. "I wish I'd never come here. This was my dad's idea when I didn't want to be on the baseball team."

Marty kicked at a pebble with his shoe. "I'm quitting. I'm taking Champ right now and never coming back."

"What about talking to your dad?" said Leanne.

"I don't need my dad. I'll adopt Champ myself."

"But you're not eighteen," said Arthur.

"So I'll fake it."

"It costs money," said Leanne.

"Then I'll steal him." Marty kicked another pebble, and it hit the front bar of the rack with a *ting*!

"Look, Marty," said Leanne. "Champ's going to be okay. The red dog was sick and he's not. Don't mess it up. Wait for your dad."

Marty pictured his dad coming home from Chicago, getting out of the car all ready to talk about Saint Bernards. When Marty told him about the freezer, he'd hop right back in and race down to the shelter for Champ.

Maybe he should wait.

"I'm gonna quit too," said Arthur. He stood up and brushed his hands against the front of his volunteer vest. "Even if I didn't like baseball, at least nobody died."

Leanne shoved the rag back into her pocket. "Oh, great. You both quit. That'll solve everything."

"You mean you'd stay?" said Marty.

"And be in the same building with that freezer?" said Arthur.

Leanne jammed her fists on her hips. "What about all the other animals? Like the new kittens? Or the mother dogs? If everybody quit, who'd take care of them?"

Marty sighed. He felt like a punching bag that was all out of stuffing. "I hate people who leave their animals here," he said.

"I hate Chris," grumbled Arthur. "He's probably the one who does it."

Leanne shook her finger first at Arthur, then at Marty. "Just because people have to give up their animals doesn't mean they want to." She spit the words out, and both boys tried to back away.

"When we moved from Kansas, I couldn't take my Jupiter. Do you think I didn't care? Do you think that was fun?

"It was too long a drive and too hot in the car and Dad didn't know exactly where we'd end up. We cried all the way through Missouri. We still miss her."

Marty stared down at his shoes.

"And don't blame Chris, either." She turned to Arthur. "I bet he gets sick every time he has to do it."

They went silent then, all three.

Marty thought about Chris actually doing it. New tears stung his eyes.

"Whose fault is it then?" said Arthur. "I know it's not ours. But whose is it?"

Leanne sniffed, her anger gone. "How should I know?"

More people came out of the shelter then. A family with a mom and a dad and two kids. The boy was carrying a kitten in his arms. The girl had a bag of food and a dish and a jingle toy.

The dad opened the car's rear door. "This was a great idea, kids," Marty heard him say. "I'm glad you suggested it."

Marty let the father's words roll around in his mind as he watched them drive out of the parking lot. He tapped his fingers against his handlebar grips. "It wouldn't matter whose fault it was," he said, thinking out loud, "if we could stop it."

"Yeah," said Arthur.

"Fat chance," said Leanne.

"But what if we could?" Marty turned to Leanne, then to Arthur. "If we found a way, would you do it?"

"Sure," said Arthur.

"There isn't a way," said Leanne.

"Maybe there is," said Marty. "If we told kids what

really happens here, they'd want to stop it. They'd get their families to adopt the animals."

Leanne shook her head.

Arthur, on the other hand, looked hopeful.

"Between the three of us," said Marty, letting the idea grow, "we could tell every kid in Johnson Falls."

"Parents don't always listen to their kids, Marty," said Leanne. "You know that."

Marty swung his leg off the bike and stood to face Leanne and Arthur. "They would this time."

"Yeah," said Arthur. "My dad would."

"If we got all the animals adopted . . ." Marty lifted his arms as if he were holding an invisible bow and arrow. He aimed at the building and let it fly. "We could shut the place down."

"YES!" hollered Arthur.

"Not possible," said Leanne.

Marty stared at her. "I thought you were the one who didn't want to quit. Now you don't even want to try?"

"Well, sure, but—"

"But what?" Marty folded his arms across his chest. "We can't succeed if we don't try."

"I'll try," said Arthur. "I know a lot of kids."

Leanne slid one foot back and forth across the blacktop.

"Leanne." Marty waited until she looked up at him. "If you'd thought of this, to find a home for Jupiter, you would have done it, wouldn't you?"

Leanne smoothed her bangs back away from her eyes. "Of course."

"Well, okay then."

They came in from the parking lot to get their lunches. They walked into the lobby, past the office, and although Marty heard Chris on the phone, he wasn't ready to look at him. So he kept his eyes straight ahead. In the kitchen he picked up his backpack.

"I'll meet you outside," he said to Leanne and Arthur. "I have to do something first."

He walked down the hall, again keeping his gaze straight ahead, safely away from the door that read STAFF ONLY. When he reached the laundry room, he marched in and scooped his turtle pillow off the counter. He unzipped his pack and stuffed it in.

Then he headed for kennel room B.

He stood in front of Champ's stall, and while Champ leaped and jumped on the inside, Marty read again the note he'd written on Champ's "Adopt ME!" card.

*This dog is reserved. Marty Igler will adopt soon.*

He pulled a pencil out of the side pouch of his pack and added: *Even if he's sick.*

How he wished he could sign his real name! Because people around town (those who knew his dad or his sister or his mom) knew they could trust a Hobarth to keep a promise.

But he couldn't. Not yet.

He dropped the pencil back into the pouch and

opened Champ's stall door. When the dog stepped out, Marty wrapped his arms around him. "You're not going to die, Champ," he whispered into the fur of one ear. "I promise."

Then he led the dog outside to the nearest fenced yard. Leanne and Arthur were waiting on the bench. They sat with their lunches.

Nobody except Champ, it turned out, was hungry.

While he ate, they made plans. Drastic plans.

They were going to cover the city from one end to the other. They'd tell every kid in Johnson Falls. So many lives would be saved, it would make the rescue show on television look like a game of tiddlywinks.

They began that afternoon.

When their volunteer shifts were over, they left the shelter together. Marty and Arthur followed Leanne as she led the way to the Walking Billboards advertising agency, one of the businesses she'd visited when she first arrived in Johnson Falls. The place that promised to put anything on the front of a T-shirt.

They parked their bikes out front and went in.

They stood under the fronds of a potted palm as they waited for the lady receptionist to get off the phone.

"Yes? May I help you?" she asked.

Marty explained about all the animals at the shelter needing homes. "We have to get everybody adopted," he said.

"Even hamsters," said Arthur.

"It's life or death," said Leanne.

The woman looked stricken, her face pale. "I love animals," she said. "My dog Pixie sleeps with me every night."

"We need to advertise," said Leanne, and she pulled a shelter brochure out from her pocket and pointed to the drawing of the animals under the umbrella on the front. "Could we get T-shirts with this picture on them? That way people will know where we're from."

"We need a message on them too. Something like 'Save a life—adopt an animal.' " Marty held his fingers far apart to show her how big the lettering should be.

The woman hesitated. She glanced around, first to one side, then the other, as if they'd just asked her to be part of a secret mission. "I'll tell you what," she said, leaning over her desk toward them. "I'll run off fliers for you. They'd work even better than shirts. How would that be?"

"That'd be fine," said Marty.

She held out a piece of paper. "Write exactly what you want to say."

Marty took the paper and a pen and, after a short discussion with Leanne and Arthur about not leaving anyone out, wrote:

*DOGS AND CATS AND OTHERS*
*WILL DIE*
*UNLESS YOU HELP*
*Adopt some at Mid-State Animal Shelter NOW!!!*

The woman pointed to a couch in the lobby. "Have a seat," she said. "It'll be a few minutes." She took the paper from Marty and disappeared down a hallway.

They flipped pages of magazines. They looked at the plants. At one point Arthur leaned back and put his feet up on the table until Leanne told him he'd better not. Marty stared out the window and thought about the red dog. His fingertips could still feel the chilled plastic of the garbage bag.

When the woman returned, she cradled a stack of papers thicker than three phone books in her arms. "If you run out," she said, "come back." She set the stack on the coffee table.

Marty looked down at the top sheet. The paper was bright, the words big and bold. And at the bottom was the umbrella picture.

It was perfect.

"Thanks," he said.

"From all of us," said Leanne.

"The hamsters, too," said Arthur.

Marty picked up the top third of the stack. He was glad he'd brought his backpack.

"Be careful," said the woman. "And good luck."

Back on the sidewalk, after they'd stuffed the fliers into their packs, Marty held out his right hand like you do before a big game.

Leanne and Arthur topped it with their own.

"Nobody quits," he said. "Deal?"

"Deal," Leanne and Arthur agreed.

"No matter how long it takes," said Marty.

"Until everybody gets adopted," added Arthur.

They shook on it.

"This could be a major thing." Leanne tightened the pink band of her ponytail. "We ought to call it something."

"Yeah," said Arthur. "Let's give it a code name."

They settled on Operation Shutdown.

# 15

# Operation Shutdown

**W**ith their packs full of fliers and their plan firmly set, Marty and Leanne and Arthur pumped down the sidewalk on their bikes like soldiers on a mission.

Three times they stopped, when they saw groups of kids, and told them about Operation Shutdown. They passed out fliers.

"Save a life," they said. "Adopt an animal."

The response was immediate.

Not only did the kids listen, but some of them, including a girl gliding by on Rollerblades, offered to hand out fliers too.

Marty's confidence soared.

Plus everybody, it seemed, needed to talk about their own pets: who had what, and how many, for how long.

It took a while.

Politely Marty and Leanne and Arthur listened until, in the middle of a cat-up-a-tree story, Marty peeked at Leanne's watch.

It was getting late, and he still had to hit the boulevard sprinklers.

"That's interesting," he said to the boy with the

128

Siamese climber. "But we have to go." He nudged Leanne.

"Yes, and thanks!" said Leanne.

"Save a life!" added Arthur.

They hopped on their bikes. Arthur headed west. Marty and Leanne waved to him and then turned south toward home. They pedaled like fiends down the avenues and across the streets, slowing only for baby strollers, stopping only at intersections. When Leanne turned onto the road that led to the apartments, Marty nodded his good-bye.

By the time he sailed past the tall pines on the corner of Fox Lane, his neighborhood was quiet. There were no more kids on the street.

It was dinnertime.

He swerved into his driveway, dropped his bike in the garage, and took the back steps two at a time. His hair, still wet from the sprinkler, was plastered to his forehead. He rubbed at it with his beach towel, opened the kitchen door, and walked in.

Dinner was on the table.

He slid into his chair. Mrs. Prinzig's meatballs, sitting in the center of his mother's blue serving platter, were the size of golf balls. Ordinarily he ate three. But tonight, when he considered the magnitude of Operation Shutdown and the effort it was going to require, and as he listened to the rumbling in his stomach, he put four of them on his plate. No, five. Who knew when he'd find time to eat another meal?

"How was your day, Francine?" asked Mrs. Prinzig as she settled herself into her chair.

"A-g-o-n-y," spelled Francine. "Agony. I studied the wrong vocab list last night and Hartzell, the creep who sits behind me, laughed all morning."

Marty reached for the bowl of mashed potatoes. He was glad Mrs. Prinzig had cooked so much.

"And you, Marty?"

Marty looked up.

"What did you do today?" Mrs. Prinzig smiled.

Marty smiled back as he scooped out a clump of potatoes with the serving spoon. How he wished he could tell them! But as he watched Francine slice the lone meatball on her plate into proper, tidy chunks, his instinct said not yet.

"Same ol' thing," he answered. He gave the spoon a shake, and the potatoes plopped onto his plate.

"Marty doesn't do much, Mrs. P.," said Francine. "My parents get mad at him a lot."

Mrs. Prinzig gave Francine a look. "Now, dear."

"It's true, Mrs. P. Really."

Marty reached for the gravy. Pretty soon Francine was going to eat her words. Spell 'em, then eat 'em. He drizzled gravy over his meatballs and imagined her gagging on a capital K or a W. He pictured her choking, begging for his help, when the phone rang and she popped up to get it.

"It never fails," said Mrs. Prinzig. "You no more than get the food laid out."

"Marty?" Francine held the receiver, her face quizzical. "It's a girl."

Marty got up.

It was Leanne.

"I still think we should have T-shirts, Marty." Her voice came fast. "I'm going to make one for myself and one for you and hopefully one for Arthur. What color do you want?"

Out of the corner of his eye, Marty saw Francine picking at her food. Picking, he knew, because she was listening. Francine was not big on privacy—other people's, that is.

"Doesn't matter," he said to Leanne.

"Aunt Jen's taking me to the craft store at the mall. She's going to help. Isn't that sweet?"

"Sure." Now Francine was watching him. He turned his back to her and stared at the cupboard.

Leanne was rattling on. "Marty, I've been thinking about Jupiter. The worst part was, I never knew what happened to her. If she got adopted or what. I should have done all this for her. Why didn't I think of it?"

Marty ran his thumbnail along a scratch in the cupboard door. He could feel Francine's eyes, like radar, at his back.

"Marty?" said Leanne. "Are you there?"

"Yeah. I'm eating."

"You should have told me you were having dinner."

"I just did."

Leanne said she was sorry to interrupt. But did he want blue or beige?

Marty said either one, thanks, and good-bye. He hung up the phone and sat back down to the table.

"Who was it?" asked Francine.

"It?" Marty stuck his fork into the spongy center of one meatball and lifted it off his plate. "Nobody you know."

● ● ●

One thing about Mrs. Prinzig—she didn't care if you helped with the dishes. So after Marty sucked the last drop of gravy and the last spot of potato off his finger, he carried his plate to the sink and grabbed his backpack.

"Thanks for dinner, Mrs. P.," he said. He walked out of the kitchen and climbed the stairs.

Francine followed. "You *are* up to something, aren't you? Don't tell me you're not, because I know you are."

Marty shuffled into his room and let the pack drop onto his bed. "If you know I am, why are you asking?"

"Because I'm the oldest and I think I ought to know what it is." She stood over him like a mother. "And what's in the pack?"

"None of your business."

"You are such a pain," she huffed.

He flopped down on his quilt. "It runs in the f-a-m-i-l-y."

"Jerk."

Marty watched her turn and stalk across the floor. He watched her grab the doorknob and yank. When the door slammed, his curtains billowed. Godzilla disappeared under the electric rock.

If she just wasn't so pushy all the time, he probably would have told her . . . even though it felt good to know something she didn't.

He leaned back against his elbow. He'd tell her later. When Operation Shutdown really got rolling and she couldn't wreck it. Or take it over.

He kicked off his shoes and let them drop on the rug. In just a few days Champ would be sleeping there. Only inches from the bed. He ought to be thinking about *that* instead of wasting his time on Francine.

He sat cross-legged and pulled the backpack over the quilt. He unzipped it and carefully, so as not to crumple the fliers, eased the turtle pillow out. He hugged it to his chest, remembering the morning he'd given it to the red dog. She'd been cautious at first. It had taken her a while to trust.

A while to trust *him.*

He pressed the pillow against his cheek and squeezed his eyes shut.

"Beautiful red lady," he whispered, his voice hoarse. "I should have done all this for you. Why didn't I think of it?"

◉ ◉ ◉

The next morning when Marty pedaled into the parking lot of the Jiffy Mart, Leanne was waiting. She had her new T-shirt on. It was pink.

"So what do you think, Marty?" she asked when he rolled to a stop.

On the shirt front was the umbrella picture, bright with colors. When she turned, he saw the back. Large letters said SAVE A LIFE—ADOPT AN ANIMAL.

"It's nice."

"Nice?" Leanne sounded insulted. "It's wonderful. We worked real hard." Her face softened. "Aunt Jen said if she could have a daughter, it would be me."

Marty was anxious to get going, so he said, "You're right. It's wonderful."

She handed him the shirt they'd made for him. It was blue. Marty said thanks and unzipped his pack to stuff it in.

"Aren't you going to put it on?"

"I will when I get there."

●　●　●

He did.

Chris was cradling the basket puppy in his arms when Marty and Leanne walked in. When he and Nancy and the rest of the staff saw the shirts, they were thrilled.

Little did they know, thought Marty as they turned him around to read the message on the back, that pretty soon they'd be out of work. Pretty soon, if everything went right, their jobs would be gone.

And everything was going to go right. He knew it. He expected it. He'd spent most of last night picturing it: empty cages, happy animals, boards nailed across the front door, and a huge sign plastered across the building that said CLOSED FOREVER.

He watched the basket puppy, her eyes closed, drink from the baby bottle in Chris's hand. I mean, that's what you were supposed to do, wasn't it? Expect success?

Of course it was.

And it wasn't as hard to do, he found, when he was away from home. Which worked out fine, because in the next days he was hardly home at all.

Each afternoon, when he and Leanne and Arthur finished their duties at the shelter, they combed the neighborhoods. They used Leanne's map and found streets that even she had not seen. They talked to kids on bikes and kids on skateboards, kids in driveways and kids on front porches. They found them at lemonade stands, in tree forts, sitting on curbs, mowing lawns. At St. Ita's Home for Children, over on the east side, everybody on the playground promised to help.

As Marty predicted, they ran out of fliers.

"There's two guys in my neighborhood," said Arthur as the three of them stood out front of Walking Billboards, stuffing the new batch of fliers into their packs. "You gotta meet 'em. They're putting these things up all over the place."

"Like where?" asked Marty.

"Like everyplace. Restaurants. Banks. The bus

station. The hospital. Even the pet store in the mall took one."

"Wow," said Leanne. "Who are they?"

"Guys on my old baseball team. Grady and the Bug." Arthur swung one leg over his bike and climbed on.

"Grady and the who?" asked Marty.

"The Bug. You gotta meet 'em."

They pushed off and went back to work. And it was work. No magic from the fortune cookie this time, thought Marty as he took a minute on the corner of Lincoln and Twenty-fifth to rub the muscles in his legs. Just a lot of hard work.

In the evenings he could barely keep his eyes open to eat Mrs. Prinzig's dinners. He was too tired to fight with Francine or even to catch crickets under the porch. Godzilla and the tree frogs were on mealworms.

But it was paying off.

Each day the shelter was crowded with visitors. Chris and Nancy were so busy, they bumped into each other coming and going.

"What in the world is happening?" Marty overheard Chris say to Nancy once.

"I don't know," she answered. "But I love it."

So did Marty. Each time he saw an animal escorted out of the shelter to a new home, he felt proud. If only people would stop bringing in new ones, Operation Shutdown would be almost done by now.

The day before his father was due home from Chicago, Marty stood with a broom and dustpan in the corner of the lobby and watched the flurry of activity.

On the shelf above the office door, the golden trophies gleamed down at him. He'd forgotten all about them. They certainly wouldn't give him one now—for putting the shelter out of business.

He steadied the dustpan and made a large swipe with the broom.

Well, so what? Empty cages were a lot better than a dumb trophy.

He carried the dustpan to the waste bin and dumped it. Then he stuck the broom away and walked into kennel room B.

He took an extra long time with Champ. He exercised him. He brushed him. He overdosed him with hugs.

"Tomorrow's the big day, Champ," he said. "Tomorrow my dad comes home."

Champ's eyebrows danced with the excitement in Marty's voice.

Marty knelt in front of him. "This time my dad will say yes. This time, after I explain things, he'll say, *Quick! Let's adopt Champ right now!*"

Champ tipped his head, his ears perked, and Marty knew he was listening to every word.

"Well, he might not say it exactly like that, Champ. But he'll say yes for sure."

Champ gave him a slurp on the nose.

Marty gave him a last, quick hug. Then he stood up and stepped out of the stall. "Tomorrow," he said, and he walked out the door.

He dropped his volunteer vest into the washing machine and then headed down the hall to the kitchen for his backpack. He had one more place to hand out fliers, one special place. And he'd decided, after stewing over it all week, that he needed to go there alone.

The pool.

On his way out he said good-bye to Arthur, who was feeding hamsters. He waved at Leanne, who was on her way into the cat room.

"Marty!" she called. Balancing a stack of fuzzy toilet-seat covers in her arms, she trundled toward him. "You're leaving already?"

He nodded.

"Are you sure you don't want us to come with you?"

She sounded worried. Like she didn't know if he could handle it. What did she think he was, anyway? Some scared baby?

"The pool's one of my favorite places," he answered, his voice bristly. "It'll be a piece of cake."

# 16

# Back to Krypton

The bike trip from the Mid-State Animal Shelter to the Johnson Falls Municipal Pool took longer than Marty'd expected. It didn't help that he had nobody to talk to. Or that he'd given most of his lunch, including half his meatball sandwich, to Champ. Or that the whole route seemed to be up-hill.

He tried to keep his mind on his pictures of success. The empty cages, the happy animals, the sign nailed up to the shelter that said CLOSED FOREVER.

But it wasn't easy.

If only he could stop at home and raid the refrigerator. Food would help. But then he'd see Mrs. Prinzig and maybe Francine. They'd want to know what he was doing there, in the middle of the day, dry instead of wet, wearing his SAVE A LIFE T-shirt.

It wouldn't be worth it.

At the corner of Buchanan he turned left. The wind gusted through his hair. It pushed against his chest. He wondered, as he pumped, if maybe it was trying to keep him from getting there. Warn him even.

It was a dumb idea.

He shook it away and pedaled on past the entrance to the Heights apartment complex. He wished he had let Leanne come along at least partway, for company. Or Arthur.

But no. He'd acted like going back to the pool was some sort of test that he had to do alone. Like Superman returns to planet Krypton, the Zilch must return to the pool.

Which was, he realized now, an even dumber idea.

The fact was, he'd rather hand out fliers on Krypton. The diving team wouldn't be there. Or everybody else who'd watched him bomb his tryout.

He looked both ways, then pedaled across Buchanan. He braced himself as his front tire bumped up over the curb.

Of course, maybe the pool kids had forgotten about him after all this time.

Ha.

He passed a row of noisy trees, their bird residents swooping. His hands were sweaty against the handlebars, so he wiped them one at a time on his shirt. He kept pumping until he reached the boulevard intersection, and there he stopped.

On the other side of the street was the municipal park. He looked across at the walking trails and the pond, the picnic area with its tables and hot-dog grills, and then up the sloping lawn to the pool itself.

Sweat broke along his forehead.

Actually Leanne and Arthur should have done this instead of him. The pool kids would listen better to them.

But if he left, Leanne would think he was a baby for sure.

He talked himself across the intersection. "This isn't a problem, Hobarth. It's an opportunity. Put a smile on. Act like a winner."

In the parking lot he steered between the rows of cars. He swerved around a group of mothers with kids whose pool toys squeaked, and aimed for the bike rack.

Maybe there wasn't room for his bike. He could always come back some other time.

But there was one slot on the end, empty and waiting. He climbed off and shoved his bike in.

Next to him was the row of bushes he'd hidden in the last time he was there. The one with all the bugs and the perfumy purple flowers. Just smelling it made his neck itch.

The noise from the pool, even from there, was loud. The splashing and the hollering and the blaring radios. Everybody was still having fun.

It had only been a few weeks since he'd been there, but it seemed like years. He hadn't missed it for a minute.

He took a deep breath and faced the sidewalk steps. Slowly he began to climb them. He was nearly halfway up when he heard the *thunk* of the diving board and it stopped him. His mind swirled.

Who was going to listen to a zilch anyway? Certainly not David. Or the other divers. They'd just laugh at him. How fun would that be?

He hadn't thought about any of this!

Plus he wasn't feeling well at all. He was dizzy. He might faint. What if somebody had to call an ambulance?

He ought to go home. He ought to quit before it was too late.

He turned his back to the pool and faced the steps he'd just climbed. Once he got away from all the noise and the bad memories and the stink of the bushes, he'd feel better. He took a step down and wiped perspiration off his forehead. His feet teetered on the edge of the next stair.

Okay, so he was quitting. Big deal. Why not? Who cared? He'd done it a million times. If only everybody would leave him alone instead of pushing him to do things all the time, maybe he could stop quitting.

But who was pushing this time?

He tried to take another step down, but the question stood in front of him like an invisible grownup.

He turned away.

Next to the sidewalk was a large oak, its limbs full with summer green. He reached up and snapped off one bright leaf. He stared at it, then punched a hole in it with his thumb.

Nobody was pushing him this time.

This time it was all his own idea. This time he'd made promises. To Champ and the other animals at the shelter. To Leanne and Arthur. To the red dog.

He kicked at a pebble on the step and sent it spinning. What would happen if he quit this time?

It didn't take a gifted student to answer that one. If he quit this time, he wouldn't even want to look in the mirror.

He slumped down on the step, his eyes stinging as if they had a whole day's worth of chlorine in them. He sniffed back a drip in his nose.

He couldn't go in there and face those kids again. He just couldn't. But he couldn't quit, either. If only there was some middle way.

He wiped his nose with the back of his arm.

What if he handed out just one flier? He could handle one kid laughing at him, couldn't he? Or two? That wouldn't be quitting. It would be, well, just not finishing. And that wasn't so bad, under the circumstances. I mean, doing something was better than doing nothing, wasn't it? At least then he'd be able to tell Leanne he'd handed out fliers. He wouldn't even have to go in.

Yes, he could do two.

He stood up and glanced around to see if anyone had noticed him sitting there acting like a baby, but there was no one. How lucky that he'd come alone!

He turned himself around and climbed the rest of the steps to the pool entrance. Ignoring the splashing and the hollering and the *thunk*ing of the board, he walked up to the creaky turnstile and dropped his pack on the ground. He unzipped it and pulled out two fliers.

When the first two kids walked through the pool exit, he handed them each a flier.

"There's trouble," he said, waiting for the laughing to start. "Can you help?"

But the kids didn't laugh. Instead their faces filled with worry. They had questions. While he answered them, several more swimmers came through the turnstile and stopped. They wanted to know what was going on, too. So Marty reached into his pack for a few more fliers.

Soon he was surrounded with dripping, worried kids.

"Where is the shelter?" a boy with goggles wanted to know.

"When is it open?" asked another.

"Every day nine to five," said Marty. He nodded to the north. "It's by the city dump. You can't miss it."

When two girls from the diving team came by, Marty heard them giggle. He handed them fliers anyway.

When David appeared, twirling the end of his beach towel, Marty hardly had time to flinch.

"We all figured your dad would make you come back and try it over again, Hobarth," David said. "Where you been?"

"Working." Marty handed him a flier.

David scanned it. "They'll die? Come on. How would you know?"

"I saw it."

David blanched.

Someone tapped Marty on the shoulder with another question, and when he turned back, David was gone.

Marty stayed by the turnstile until the miraculous happened. All his fliers were gone. In a daze he scooped up his pack, which now weighed barely anything at all, and headed for the steps.

David was standing by the big oak. "Hobarth," he said when Marty walked past.

Marty stopped. "What?"

"I don't get it." David held up his flier. "Wouldn't you rather be on a team than doing this?"

Marty hooked his backpack over one shoulder and smiled. That was an easy one. "No way, Dave. *No way*. See ya."

He bounced down the steps to the bike rack. He'd done it. And it really had been a piece of cake. His dad had been right all along. If a guy didn't quit, he could do anything. The only trick was, you had to want it bad enough.

# 17

# Discoveries

**M**arty realized as he rode the breeze home from the pool that he'd just made a discovery. An important, change-your-life discovery.

He wasn't a zilch anymore. Why, he'd probably never actually been one. It was just that he didn't like to dive. In fact, he *hated* diving. Even with nose plugs.

He pumped down the boulevard and thought about how he didn't like hockey all that much either. Or basketball. They were fun to play now and then, but every day for hours?

No wonder he always bombed his tryouts. I mean, how could you be a winner at something you didn't like?

It made perfect sense.

As he sailed past the stand of white pines on the corner of Fox Lane, he raised his arms like wings for balance and rode no hands. He felt good. No, he felt great. Like his mother must feel when she finally found something in the dirt. Or his dad when he ran a race. Or maybe even Francine when she spelled some word right.

He thought of all the animals getting adopted at the shelter. Animals that wouldn't end up in the freezer. All because of Operation Shutdown.

He put his hands back on the grips and guided his front tire through a patch of sand. "I'm better than a diver," he announced as he rounded the last curve in the road. "I'm a death fighter."

He ought to congratulate himself.

When he reached his own driveway, he saw that Mrs. Prinzig's car was gone. He did a lazy figure eight across the blacktop before he rolled his bike into the garage.

He couldn't wait to tell her. And even Francine. As soon as his dad got home from Chicago the next day, he'd sit them down and tell them everything. At the very end, he'd announce his discovery. They were going to be so proud. It was going to be wonderful.

He parked his bike and gave it a pat on the handlebars. A pat for all the miles, for all the help.

On his way into the house, he stopped by his mother's geraniums and picked three. Because flowers meant somebody'd done something special.

He bounced up the back steps and reached for the screen-door handle.

It was locked from the inside.

Francine, he saw, was in the kitchen.

He held the geraniums behind his back. "Francine! Open up."

She blew a large purple gum bubble as she ambled toward the door. When the bubble popped, she pulled the gum off her cheek and stuffed it back into her mouth. "Well, well," she said. "If it isn't Mr. Lie-Every-Minute."

"Mr. what?"

She stood inside the door, gum clacking, and he could smell grape through the screen.

"Lie, Marty. You know. L-I-E. The opposite of truth."

"Huh?"

"I followed you this morning when you left for your diving practice. Only you didn't go to your diving practice. You met some girl at the Jiffy Mart. I was behind you all the way to the river bridge before I had to get to school." She folded her arms and looked down at him. "I don't know what you're up to, but whatever it is, it's not at the pool."

Marty jiggled the handle. "I can explain."

"Don't bother." She took a step back from the door as if she were leaving. "Guess what else I found out? You're not even on the diving team. Ann Louise Miller's sister told me you flunked your tryout. You lied to me and to Mrs. Prinzig and even to Dad. I bet you lied to Mom, too, in your letter. That's sick, Marty."

He let the flowers drop and yanked at the door with both hands. "It's not like that, Francine. Open up. I can explain."

She wasn't listening. "When Mrs. Prinzig finds out, she'll cry. She thinks you're nice. Mom will be devastated."

Marty stamped his foot. "Francine! Lemme in!"

"But Dad will be the worst." She slashed her index finger across her neck. "I hate to think!"

Just then a car rolled into the drive. Marty turned. It was Mrs. Prinzig.

"Groceries!" she called, through the open window. "Come help me, kids!"

Marty turned back to Francine. He pressed his fingers to the screen. "Don't tell her. Please. I'll give you whatever you want. Just let *me* tell her."

Francine tapped her fingers against her cheek.

"Pleeease, Francine. I'm going to tell everybody tomorrow anyway. I'll give you anything you want."

"Anything?"

He hated to do it. "Anything."

"I shouldn't, really." She unlocked the door and stepped out. "You're probably in a big mess."

"Come on, Francine," he pleaded.

"Oh, all right. I'll do it for five bucks."

"Five bucks! That's almost all I have."

She shrugged. "Oh, Mrs. P.!"

"Okay, okay! Five bucks."

They hauled grocery bags while Mrs. Prinzig talked. "Your dad called. He's coming home early. Before dinner tonight. Won't that be nice?"

"Real nice," said Francine.

When Marty shuffled past her, carrying milk cartons, she did the slashing-finger thing again.

He shoved the cartons into the refrigerator and then raced up the stairs to his room. He dug through his bottom drawer and pulled out the small metal safe. He fumbled for the combination, and when the little door popped open, he pulled out 5 one-dollar bills. He needed to hurry, before big-mouth changed her mind.

He grabbed her outside the kitchen. "Here," he said. "Take it. Just keep your mouth shut till dinner. I'll tell everybody then."

"They're gonna E-X-P-L-O-D-E," she said as she folded the bills and stuck them in her pocket. "No matter what I don't say."

"You're wrong, Francine. It's not like that. You'll see. You'll all see."

◉ ◉ ◉

Mr. Hobarth arrived with gifts.

"For my troops!" he said as he walked into the kitchen. His arms were full with packages, his suitcase, his thermos for coffee. "Miss me?"

"Totally," said Francine, setting the table for dinner. She gave her dad a hug and then turned to Marty. "Marty was lonesome too."

Marty, helping with the silverware, said, "Yeah, Dad. Totally." He was almost afraid to look in his dad's face. Had he found the note in his glove box? Was he ready to hear the truth? What if he acted like Francine and wouldn't listen?

He set the forks on the table in a clump. What he needed was to sneak off to his room and calm down. It was all happening so fast!

Before he could escape, his dad asked them all to

sit down. He gave both Francine and Marty beach towels. "For our trip to the lake," he said.

Then he gave them Cubs baseball caps. Mrs. Prinzig got one too. They all put them on and looked at each other in the blue hats, and laughed when Mrs. Prinzig's slid down over her puffy hair and covered one eye.

"You're all such dears," she said.

It was like a small party—with everyone in such a good mood. Marty looked at the bright orange geraniums that Mrs. Prinzig had rescued and put in a vase on the table, and wished his mother was there. Then he could tell her at dinner too, and she wouldn't be devastated.

"What's been going on here?" asked Mr. Hobarth, adjusting his cap.

"The children have been so busy," said Mrs. Prinzig, "I've hardly seen them."

"Marty too?" Mr. Hobarth smiled.

"Especially Marty," said Francine.

Marty shot her a murderous glare.

"What's up, Mart?" Mr. Hobarth leaned forward. "I bet the diving's going great."

"He won't tell us until dinner," said Francine with a pout. "It's some big secret."

Marty shifted in his chair. He wished he could punch her to the moon—after he got his five dollars back. He looked up from the geraniums. Both his dad and Mrs. Prinzig were waiting.

"It's not that big," he said.

They were still at the kitchen table when the doorbell rang.

Francine jumped up to get it.

"Marty," she said when she came back to the kitchen. "It's somebody for you. A man."

A man?

Marty got up and pushed open the swinging kitchen door. He took two steps down the hall and stopped.

It was Chris from the shelter, outside the screen door.

But how? He didn't have Marty's right address, or phone number, or even his right last name. Somehow he'd found out about the lies.

Marty felt his face flush. Hesitantly he stepped up to the door. "Chris?"

"Hi, Marty."

"What are you doing here?"

"I came to see you. Can we talk?"

Marty chewed at the inside of his lip and thought of the little party in the kitchen. He heard his dad laugh. This was not the time to talk to Chris!

"We're kinda busy right now," he said sheepishly. "My dad just got home from an important trip. Could you come back tomorrow?"

Tomorrow he'd tell Chris everything. Tomorrow he'd even ask him to join the party!

But before Chris could answer, Marty heard the kitchen door swing open behind him.

"Marty?" It was his dad.

Marty wished he could faint. He watched his dad, still wearing his Cubs hat, step up to the door.

"Um, Dad," he squeaked. "This is Chris. He was just leaving."

His dad wasn't listening. "I'm John Hobarth," he said in his best make-the-customer-feel-welcome voice. "How can we help you?"

"Marty said you've just returned home. I don't want to interrupt."

Marty sighed with relief.

But his dad said, "Nonsense. Come on in." He opened the door.

The two men shook hands, and Marty began to sweat.

"I'm Chris Schroers, Mr. Hobarth. Your son is one of my favorite kids."

"Mine too." Mr. Hobarth smiled. "You must be coaching Marty's diving team."

Marty's legs went to Jell-O. He was never going to lie again! Not even for a good reason!

"Well, actually," said Chris, with a look to Marty. "I'm the manager of the animal shelter."

"Excuse me?"

"Marty is one of my volunteers."

Mr. Hobarth's eyebrows furrowed. "I'm afraid I don't follow."

"I was afraid you wouldn't," said Chris.

"I was going to tell you, Dad." Marty's voice was still only a squeak. Nobody seemed to even hear it. He wiped the palms of his hands against his shirt.

The kitchen door swung open then and Francine's head poked out, her eyes bugged.

"Let's talk in the den," said Mr. Hobarth. With a quick shake of his head at Francine, he led the way down the hall.

Marty forced himself to follow behind Chris, past the awards cabinet with its trophies and ribbons and the giant silver cup that gleamed in the sunlight from the hall window.

They filed into the den. It was cool and quiet at the back end of the house. The slats of the window blinds, half closed against the sun, let in only narrow lines of light. Mr. Hobarth closed the door and turned on the pole lamp. He motioned for Chris to sit in the rocking chair. Then he leaned against the edge of the desk, took off his Cubs hat, and folded his arms across his chest.

Marty stood on the sample carpet. "I was going to tell you, Dad," he said again lamely. "Honest."

"Then tell me now."

Marty looked down at the brown speckles in the carpet and tried to think of exactly where to start. He tried to remember about his discovery. But his brain felt like mush.

"Marty." His dad was losing patience.

Marty shoved his hands into his pockets. He could start with Champ. Sure. That was a good idea. "Remember the dog you took to the shelter, Dad? The one who tried to eat your sunglasses?"

His father frowned.

Marty swallowed. He had to keep going no matter how unhappy his dad looked. So, skipping the part about the dive, he began with how he'd gone to the shelter to save Champ. How he'd seen the other dogs. But it wasn't easy. Every time he said something, his dad said "Hold it a minute" and stopped him for details. He asked questions. Marty got confused.

"Who's this Igler girl?" his father asked. "I've never heard that name before."

"She's not from here."

"Oh? Then where did you meet her?"

"In a parking lot."

"Parking lot! For heaven's sake, Marty."

Marty blew air out of his mouth to cool his face. This was going to go on forever.

"I don't understand how you could even be a volunteer without my permission. Doesn't the shelter have rules?"

"We faked the application. We pretended I was Leanne's brother." Marty glanced quickly up at Chris. "But it was all my idea. I made her do it."

Mr. Hobarth sat shaking his head. "For heaven's sake, Marty," he said for the umpteenth time.

Chris cleared his throat. "It happens sometimes, Mr. Hobarth. Kids want to work with the animals even if their parents say no. My fault in this is I neglected to verify the application. It looked like everything was in order, and I got busy with other things."

"Do you have it with you? I'd like to see it."

"Yes." Chris opened the folder in his lap and pulled the application out. Slowly, as if he was sorry he had to do it, he passed the paper to Mr. Hobarth.

Marty stood in the center of the room like a convict in handcuffs and waited while his dad held the paper under the light of the pole lamp and read it.

Why hadn't he listened to Leanne and just told his dad the truth? Or better yet, why hadn't he just tried the dive over again until he got it right?

"If it's at all possible, Mr. Hobarth," said Chris, "I'd like to work this out. Marty's one of my best volunteers."

"I don't know." Mr. Hobarth dropped the application on the desk like it was something he didn't want to touch. He gave Marty a withering look. "How could you do this, Marty? Haven't we taught you to tell the truth?"

Marty fastened his eyes on a small bug who, with tremendous effort, was straining to climb the fibers of the carpet.

"Answer me, Marty. Why didn't you come to me?"

"You would have said no."

"And with good reason!" Mr. Hobarth thwapped the baseball cap against his knee. "Your job this summer is at the pool."

Marty let his feet sink deeper into the carpet. "I haven't been to the pool, Dad," he said, in a whisper.

"You *what*?" Mr. Hobarth's voice filled the den.

Marty blinked, his face hot with shame. If only Chris wasn't there to hear this. "I flunked the try-out, Dad. I was afraid to tell you."

"Oh, Marty."

Marty glanced up quickly. His father's eyes were brimmed with disappointment. Chris, sitting like a statue, wouldn't look at him at all.

Marty jammed his hands to the very bottom of his pockets and waited for his dad to really blow. For Chris to get up and leave. To say he didn't like Marty anymore and that he didn't want a flunkee for a volunteer anyway.

But nobody said a thing. The den was so quiet, Marty could hear pans rattling in the kitchen.

When he couldn't stand the silence another second, and because it didn't matter what he said now, he told them about the cookie. About following his heart, which wanted to save dogs, instead of doing what he was supposed to, which was what everybody else wanted. He remembered about his discovery.

When he'd finished, his dad sighed a long sigh.

Marty let his shoulders sag. Like a collapsing balloon, he let the rest of the truth escape. "Our plan was to save all the animals so there'd be no more dead bodies in garbage bags and no more garbage bags in the freezer."

Chris lurched forward. "Marty, how do you know about the freezer?"

Marty told him about the hamster chase. "You

probably don't believe me, but the only reason I went in there was to get Kenny."

Chris sank back in the chair. "Now I'm beginning to understand. Operation Shutdown was your idea, wasn't it?"

"Operation Shutdown?" Mr. Hobarth sounded lost.

Marty did his best to explain.

"We've been so busy," said Chris, looking at Mr. Hobarth. "The whole staff's been working overtime just to process the papers for all the adoptions."

Chris set his folder on the floor. "What amazes me is that you kept on working after, well, after seeing the freezer. Most kids would have quit. Most *adults* would have quit."

"I almost did," said Marty. "But my dad says you can't succeed if you quit. So Leanne and Arthur and me, we promised each other we wouldn't. Not until all the animals had homes. We wanted to shut the place down."

"And put us out of a job, eh?" There was a lightness in Chris's voice that sounded like a tease.

Marty looked up.

"It's all right, Marty. I wish that part of our job would disappear too. Our community-service programs could keep us more than busy."

Marty chanced a look over at his dad. He was staring off, turning his cap in his lap.

Chris cleared his throat. "There's another reason I'm here, Marty. It's how I discovered all this today."

There was more?

"Late this afternoon a family came in to see the Bernard cross. The dog you called Champ."

Marty's breath caught.

"You took such great care of him, Marty. The baths, the toys, the special exercise, all the time you spent. I know he was fond of you."

*Was* fond? Marty pulled his hands out of his pockets and stood straight. Why did Chris say *was*?

"I saw the note you wrote on his card, so I knew you wanted to adopt him. But I couldn't find you. When I called the phone number on your application, Leanne's aunt answered. She didn't know anything about a dog."

Marty shook his head no.

"They adopted him, Marty."

Marty shook his head harder. A hum started in his ears. "They can't. He's mine."

"I'm sorry, Marty, but they already did."

"Then you have to get him back."

"I can't do that."

"Yes you can."

"Marty," Mr. Hobarth warned.

"But it's not fair!" Tears filled Marty's eyes as he banged his fist against his chest. "Champ belongs to *me*. I found him. He's *mine*."

Chris rose out of the chair. "Try to understand, Marty. I couldn't let the chance for an adoption slip by. For the dog's sake. And considering what's happened here today, I think it all turned out for the best."

"No!" Marty faced Chris, his heart fierce. "Get him back!"

Chris took a step toward him. "I can't. But believe me, I know how you feel."

*"You do not!"*

"Marty!" His dad stood.

Marty blinked up at the both of them, first his dad and then Chris, and he knew, suddenly, that it didn't matter what was fair. Or right. Or what he wanted. It was two against one. Adults against the kid. And they'd already decided.

His breath came fast and shallow as he backed himself across the carpet, away from them. One step, two steps, three. Until his shoulders bumped the frame of the bookcase that stood against the wall. His hands grappled for something to hold on to. His fingers slid across the spines of books as Chris's voice droned. Pleading, drifty. "Sorry, Marty, really sorry."

Marty shook his head until the narrow lines of light from the window blinds made zigzags across the bleary room. His hands gripped the books, both hands, and he began to pull them out. Heave them out. Handfuls *out*. His elbows banged against the wood.

His dad came toward him, broadstepping the room as books sailed through the air. They thunked against the side of the desk and wobbled the lamp.

"Calm down, buddy."

"Just a minute, Mart."

Mrs. Prinzig was outside the door. "Is everything all right in there, dears?"

*"NO!"* Marty roared. *"I need Champ!"*

His arms flailing, hands knotted into fists, Marty swung wild. At the air. At his dad. At Chris. Until his dad caught him and wrapped him in his arms.

And it was over.

Marty closed his eyes and collapsed against the wall of his father's chest.

Champ was gone.

# 18

# Home

**M**arty opened his eyes to the pearly half light of the moon as it streamed in through his open bedroom window. He lay atop the quilt, his head murky with sleep, and hoped that if he could just get himself to wake up, he'd know it had all been a bad dream.

He squinted up at the planets of his mini solar system, which hung gray and lifeless above him.

There wasn't even a whisper of breeze.

Something skittered up the bark of the oak tree outside his window. He tried to raise himself up, to look out, but when he did, his arm throbbed. He touched it. There was a tender, egg-shaped lump above his elbow. He sagged back against the pillow.

It hadn't been a dream.

He'd had a fight with the den. Pitching books and throwing punches, and he'd lost. He put his hand over his eyes and let the tears come.

It was all true.

Champ was gone.

"You're awake." It was his dad's voice.

Marty lifted his head and looked around the room. His dad was in the shadows, behind the beam of moonlight from the window, sitting in the desk chair.

Marty let his head sink back as he listened to his dad pull the chair up to the bed.

"Marty," he said, his voice hoarse.

Marty turned his head away. Hot tears rolled onto the pillow.

"I wish your mother was here."

What could she do? Marty wanted to ask. What could anybody do? But he didn't ask. Because it didn't matter anyway. It was too late.

"She'd know what to say to you, Mart. She'd know how to help." His father sounded close to tears too. "She's always been better with you kids than I am."

Marty closed his eyes.

His dad reached over and laid his hand on Marty's. "You started to tell me, didn't you? With the note in the car. I didn't understand."

Marty shook his head on the pillow. Why talk about it now? "It's okay, Dad. It doesn't matter."

● ● ●

In the next days nothing did. So Marty sat at home.

He lugged the portable television up to his room and watched the people on *The Price Is Right* win cars and boats. He saw *Unsolved Mysteries* reruns and French cooking demonstrations and all the afternoon talk shows.

His dad postponed their trip to the lake.

Francine gave him back his five dollars.

And another postcard came from his mother: *Success, darlings! Catalogued three pieces of a cooking pot. Miss you.*

She didn't mention his letter with the dog drawing. Maybe she hadn't gotten it. Maybe he'd spelled the address wrong and the mailman in Mexico had thrown it away. Which was just fine.

Leanne came over twice to cheer him up. Once with her Aunt Jen, who said she was happy to finally meet the famous Marty. She had a ponytail like Leanne's. She invited him to visit her and Leanne at the apartment. To swim in the pool.

He thanked her for the invitation but, he said, he didn't feel much like swimming.

The second time Leanne came alone. Since television bored her, she turned it off.

"Still depressed?" she asked.

"I'm not depressed. I don't even know what it means."

"It means sitting around all day in your pajamas not caring about anything."

He shrugged.

"You gotta get over it, Marty."

He picked up the channel changer and pushed the power button. "Maybe I don't want to."

Over the noise of a laughing audience, she told him her Jupiter story again. It made him even more cranky.

When she happened to see the postcard from his mom sitting on his night table, she got cranky too.

At least he had a mom who was going to come home, she said. Hers left and didn't. "So you're not the only one who's sad, Marty."

It made him feel worse. Champ gone and the red dog gone and now Leanne's mother. "I hate it," he said.

"Me too. But it's not a good enough reason to give up." She wanted to know when he was going to get out of bed.

"Not yet."

The next afternoon he was on his quilt flipping channels when his door swung open and his dad walked in.

"You have a visitor, Marty. Come downstairs."

He hadn't heard a doorbell. And what was his dad doing home in the middle of the day? "Who is it?"

"Right now, Marty."

Marty shuffled down the stairs in his pajamas. He padded barefoot across the front hall and pushed open the kitchen door.

On the table sat a wicker laundry basket.

His dad stood off to the side and nodded for Marty to go ahead.

He took a step toward it and looked in. It was the rust-colored puppy. The one the staff at the shelter had been feeding with a bottle.

"What's she doing here?"

Mr. Hobarth leaned against the refrigerator and folded his arms. "I stopped by the shelter today. Chris said they're still so busy, they needed someone to take care of her. I said I thought you could do it."

Marty looked down at the shiny tiles in the floor. It was a setup. His dad was trying to replace Champ. "I don't want her," he said.

"You don't have to want her. When she's old enough, they'll take her back and put her up for adoption."

Marty could hardly believe it. His dad thought he could make everything all better when it was his fault it had gotten wrecked in the first place!

But it wasn't going to work.

"I thought I couldn't have a dog." Marty glared, his chest tight with blame. "You always said I couldn't have a dog. You said I couldn't have Champ. No pets, you said. What about that?"

"I was wrong." His dad kept his eyes steadily on Marty until Marty had to look away. His chest ached.

"If I can't have Champ, I don't want anybody."

"I thought you wanted to take care of animals."

"Not anymore."

"All right, Marty." Mr. Hobarth walked across the kitchen and gripped the handles of the basket. "Chris said he knew he could trust you with her. That he'd hate to lose her. But I'll tell him you're not interested."

Lose her?

A picture of the freezer flashed through Marty's mind. "Wait."

He looked into the basket again. The puppy was curled on a fuzzy toilet-seat cover, her eyes slammed shut, one leg twitching with a dream.

Marty let his shoulders slump. She didn't know that she didn't belong there. That this was Champ's house and she wasn't Champ. She didn't even know who she was. She was too little to know anything.

Marty sighed. "Okay, I'll do it. But I won't like her."

"No one's asking you to like her."

"Chris will take her back when she's ready?" Marty smoothed one finger over the puppy's soft ear.

"The very day." His dad let go of the basket handles. He stood behind Marty for a time and then walked toward the kitchen door. He was almost to the hall when Marty turned.

"Dad?"

His dad stopped in the open doorway.

"What were you doing at the shelter, anyway?"

"I wanted to see where you went when you followed your heart."

Marty had to call her something, so he picked Lady. Because she was red and it reminded him.

And all of a sudden he couldn't get rid of Francine. She wanted to tidy up messes and mix the puppy formula and wash the toilet-seat cover. She dragged in all her friends.

What a pain.

Leanne came by on her way home from the shelter to tell him Aunt Jen was getting a cat. The apartment manager had been outvoted. "I'm going to start on the other buildings now," she said. "I could sure use some help, Marty."

"I'll think about it," he answered.

They watched Lady try to chew one of the squeak toys Marty'd bought for Champ. "She's going to be beautiful, Marty."

She already was, thought Marty, although he didn't say so.

Finally, so the puppy could get some rest, he said good-bye to Leanne and took the basket up to his room. He set it on the rug next to his bed.

Which was where he was when Arthur called.

Marty trudged down the stairs to pick up the phone.

"It's urgent," said Arthur mysteriously. "Double urgent. Get over here *now*, Hobarth."

"I can't," said Marty. He was about to hang up when Arthur said the magic word.

*Champ.*

"I found him, Marty."

"Just a minute." Marty dropped the phone and ran up the stairs.

"I need to leave for a while," he said to Francine, who with three other girls was in his room cooing over the basket.

"Go," she answered. "We'll take care of Lady."

Marty flew back down to the kitchen and grabbed the phone. "Gimme directions."

◉  ◉  ◉

He pedaled fast, his heart in his throat, the directions swimming in his head, as he passed all the places Arthur told him to watch for. The bus station. The Falls Bowling Alley. Some big brick high school.

When he saw the ball field on Johnson Boulevard, he knew he was almost there, and he ground the pedals even harder. He could feel Champ getting closer with every pump.

He made one last turn, and then ahead of him was Arthur. Straddling his bike, pulling him in with a wave, right where he said he'd be. Behind a large bush on the sidewalk of Cooney Avenue.

"Hey, Marty," said Arthur.

"Hey, Arthur." Marty bent to catch his breath. His hands pulsed from gripping the handlebars.

"What are you gonna do, Marty?" Arthur no longer sounded mysterious. He sounded worried.

"Where's Champ?"

"There." Arthur leaned out from behind the bush and pointed across the street.

Marty looked up at a sprawling old house with two front doors and a porch that wrapped all the way around it. He saw toys in the grass and a small girl on the sidewalk, riding a tricycle.

He strained his eyes for any sign of Champ. He

became a human telescope, focusing on every inch of window, every foot of porch. "I don't see him. Is he inside? Where is he? How do you know he's there?"

"He got adopted by my friend Bug."

"*Who?*"

"Bug Dockerty. Remember the guys I told you about?"

"No."

"The ones who handed out all the fliers for us?"

"No."

"I know I told you."

"I don't remember."

"Well, one of them was Bug. The other one was Grady. They live over there."

A memory stirred. Marty shifted uncomfortably. But kept his eyes on the house. And as if his gaze were magnetic, one of the front doors swung open and a golden dog burst out, followed by a boy with a baseball mitt. Before the screen could slam, another boy bounced out. He had red hair and glasses.

And then came Champ.

Marty had to bite his lip to keep from hollering out. He hardly breathed as he watched the dogs romp. As he heard the boys laugh. Champ followed the boy with the glasses everywhere. They tumbled on the grass, wrestling themselves into a pile of legs and fur and sweeping tail.

Then the boys began to play catch.

"It'll never work," said Marty.

"Huh?" Arthur stepped out from behind the bush. "Champ doesn't know how to fetch."

He was right. Although the golden dog knew how to field, Champ took off with the ball every time. Marty smiled when the boy with the glasses had to run after him. He squelched a laugh when the girl on the tricycle joined the chase.

Arthur tapped his fingers on the handlebar of Marty's bike. "What are you gonna do, Marty? Champ looks happy here, and these guys are my friends. Maybe I shouldn't have called."

Marty pulled the front of his shirt away from his chest to let some air cool him. He blew out with a huff.

"I don't know yet. I gotta think."

He didn't have time. Because the boy with the golden dog had seen Arthur. He hollered hi. He started across the street.

Marty's heart soared. Except for the girl, they were all coming.

He squeezed his hand grips tight as the dogs loped across the street toward him. "Champ!" he called out.

And then Champ was in front of him, on his hind legs, and Marty let his bike fall to the sidewalk. He wrapped his arms around him, buried his face, and breathed in fur.

Arthur stood on the other side of the fallen bike, talking. Explaining. "Marty's the one who started the thing at the shelter," he said nervously. "He's the one who found Champ."

Marty looked out from the side of Champ's neck and said hi.

"Champ?" said the boy with the glasses, who was Bug. "I named him Hobo."

Hobo?

Marty frowned. "His name's Champ."

"Hey, Bug," said the boy with the golden dog, who was Grady. "I like Champ better than Hobo. I think you should pick it."

"Really?"

"Really."

Bug stepped over the bike and walked up to Marty. He put his hand on Champ's shoulder. "Hey, dog of the world. Do you want to be Hobo or do you want to be Champ?"

At the sound of Bug's voice, Champ pushed against Marty's shoulders, trying to free himself from Marty's hold. When Marty let go, Champ lunged at Bug.

Marty watched, stung.

When Champ gave Bug's glasses a slurp, a lump started in Marty's throat. He reached to touch the fringe of Champ's sweeping tail.

"Marty was going to adopt Champ," said Arthur hurriedly.

Bug stared at Marty, his eyes huge behind the wet lenses. "You were? Oh man, I'm glad you didn't. He's my first dog. My family has always had cats but they make me sneeze so I had fish instead but they're nothing like dogs. Nobody was ever like this guy!" He grinned at Champ.

"Bug," said Grady. "They don't care about that stuff."

"Oh, right. Sorry." Bug pulled his glasses off and wiped them on his droopy shirt.

Marty watched Bug with his freckles and his fire-orange hair and wished he was a mean kid. Somebody who didn't deserve a dog or know how to be nice.

But clearly that wasn't the case.

The kid was crazy about Champ. He kept making faces at him. Smiles and raised eyebrows and winks. He looked almost silly. Champ looked confused but interested.

Marty knew he ought to tell Bug why he'd biked over. That he wanted Champ back. But somehow the words wouldn't come.

"Now that Champ lives here," said Grady firmly, "maybe you could adopt somebody else."

Marty blinked. The kid was reading his mind!

"He probably will," Arthur answered, in a rush. "Right, Marty?"

Marty watched Bug nuzzle Champ.

"What about the basket puppy your dad took home?"

Marty turned sharply to Arthur. "How do you know about that?"

"I was there the day he came to the shelter. Your dad's nice. He shook my hand."

Marty groaned. All of a sudden everybody was against him. Nobody was on his side. He wished he could yell at somebody like he'd done that day in the den. Tell them this wasn't fair.

But it wouldn't do any good now, either.

Because Champ loved Bug now. Any dunce could see that. Even an ungifted dunce.

"What kind of puppy is it?" asked Grady.

"We don't know yet," said Arthur. "She's super little. Chris thinks maybe part retriever."

"Like my Tiny," said Grady, placing his hand on the head of the golden dog. "Except he's total retriever."

Marty swallowed hard as he watched Champ tug on the end of Bug's long shirt. Teasing. Playful. Happy. He watched until he couldn't stand it another second.

Abruptly he turned away, his whole body aching for Champ.

But this was what he'd always wanted, wasn't it? What he'd promised Champ from the very first? A home and somebody to belong to?

Of course it was.

But never in a million years was it supposed to turn out like this. Never with somebody else.

"When the puppy gets bigger, you could come over a lot, Marty," said Bug, yanking back his shirt. "We could do things together. We're going to make a video of the dogs and send it to that show on TV. Your puppy could be in it too."

"That would work out great!" Arthur was on the verge of relief. "You could hang around over here and meet my ferret."

Barely listening, Marty bent down for his bike. "I gotta go home," he said.

When he climbed on, Champ pranced over and then stood next to him, as if he were going along. Marty looked at Bug. His face had gone pale.

"No, Champ buddy." Marty ruffled the dog's ear. He rubbed him under the chin. "You gotta stay. This is where you live now. This is home." He wanted to say more but he couldn't. His voice was cracking and his eyes were filling up.

"Hold him, Bug," he said. And when Bug did, he shoved off.

Across the street, the small girl on the tricycle waved and blew him a kiss.

*Home.*

It was the magic word. He said it over and over as he pedaled down the street. As he thought of Champ and Bug, of Grady and his dog, together all the time, having fun.

He blinked at the sidewalk in front of him, but it blurred anyway, so he stopped on a corner by the high school and wiped at his nose with the back of one arm.

He'd feel better if he could just get home. And he *could* get home. He could do anything, he reminded himself, as long as he wanted it bad enough. One thing would help. If he could think of something besides Champ.

With a sniff he climbed back on the bike. As he pushed off, he decided to concentrate on home. On Godzilla. On the tree frogs.

But then there was Lady. The puppy everybody expected him to love.

He pumped past the bowling alley and pictured her little fuzz face. Her busy tail. Her smooth pot belly that wasn't even as big as one of Champ's paws.

And the lump in his throat came back. His eyelids stung. He tried to erase her from his mind, but she kept popping back. When he reached the hill that led down to Buchanan, he pedaled instead of gliding. The wind blasted across his face.

What was he going to do about Lady?

His dad had left the decision up to him. "We'll make room for her, Marty, if you want her."

Francine's begging had been constant. "She's perfect for us. Mom will love her too. Come on, Marty. Do something right for once."

But they didn't understand, either of them. They didn't get it at all. Lady would never be Champ.

He braked at the bottom of the hill and turned right in front of the bus station. In front of the sign that said DISCOVER AMERICA—GO GREYHOUND. It had a drawing of a dog on it. He looked away.

Riding hard, he made it home without having to stop again. When he rolled into his driveway, he saw Francine on the porch with some boy.

"Where's Lady?" he called to her.

"Sleeping, I think."

"You think? You don't know?" He knew from experience what could happen if you took your eyes off of somebody little for even a minute. He let his bike drop.

"Geez, Francine." He scowled as he bolted past her. "She only weighs five pounds."

"Well, S-O-R-R-Y!"

He swung open the front door and walked in. He saw the puppy immediately.

She was stranded, halfway up the center staircase, her front paws slipping on the shiny hardwood. Three steps below was the turtle pillow, which, compared to her, was huge. She must have been trying to haul it up or drag it down the steps.

"Lady!"

She saw him and whimpered.

He rushed up and grabbed her. "For heaven's sake, Lady! What ya trying to do, kill yourself?" He held her tight against his chest.

She struggled to reach his chin. When she did, he felt a frenzy of tiny licks. Her nails scratched at the neck of his shirt.

He closed his eyes and tried not to think about what would have happened if he hadn't come in just then. He tried not to picture her, a broken puppy at the bottom of the stairs.

"Okay, okay, it's okay. Shhh," he soothed. "Everything's gonna be okay now. I'm home."

At the sound of his words, she stopped her wriggling. He opened his eyes and saw that she was looking straight at him. As if she'd understood.

It was a shock.

He sank down on the step. "You think everything's gonna be fine just because I said so?"

Her eyes shone up at him like bright beads. It meant yes, he knew. She trusted him.

Oh, man.

He shook his head, his thoughts raw and jumbled with the events of the day. He leaned back against the step. His foot bumped the turtle pillow. He reached down and pulled it to him, rubbing the familiar smooth spot across his cheek. When he set it in his lap, Lady draped one paw across it and yawned.

"Aren't you even a little bit worried?" he asked. "I've messed a lot of things up, you know."

He watched her, to see what she thought of that, but she was already sound asleep.

# Epilogue

**THE JOHNSON FALLS *GAZETTE***
Labor Day Edition
Community News Page

### Local Boy Wins Award

The Central State Volunteer Association this week announced the winner of their Junior Volunteer of the Year Award. He is Lawrence Martin Hobarth of Johnson Falls.

Hobarth, whose family owns Hobarth's F & A, initiated the familiar "Save a life—adopt an animal" campaign, which was responsible for placing almost 200 pets in homes this summer alone. When asked his secret for success, Hobarth said there wasn't one, except to follow your heart and try to not quit. People should know, he added, that being a winner didn't mean everything was a piece of cake.

Hobarth lives with parents John and Liz Hobarth, sister Francine, three-month-old puppy Lady, and various terrarium life.

Shelter manager Chris Schroers is proud to say that Hobarth's trophy will be on display at the Mid-State Animal Shelter for one month. He invites the public to come for a visit.

Several Johnson Falls juniors, along with Hobarth, will be working at the shelter once weekly through the upcoming school year. They are: Leanne Igler (new resident), Arthur Finley, Jr., Grady Hunstiger, "Bug" Dockerty, and Elizabeth Winters.

Commendations to all these local volunteers, and special congratulations to the winner, our own champ Hobarth.

F
STR

Strommen, Judith
Bernie

94-02

Champ Hobarth

$14.45

F
STR

Strommen, Judith
Bernie

94-02

Champ Hobarth

$14.45

| DATE | BORROWER'S NAME | |
|------|-----------------|---|
| FEB 8 | Aaron M | 127 |
| FEB 15 | Aaron M | |
| APR 4 | Aaron M | 107 |
| | Hea... | |